MURDER IN GRENOBLE

BOOK 11 OF THE MAGGIE NEWBERRY MYSTERIES

SUSAN KIERNAN-LEWIS

SAN MARCO PRESS

Swept Away
Carried Away
Stolen Away

The French Women's Diet

1

THE NIGHTS GROW COLDER

Maggie snuggled down under the duvet, resisting the moment when she would have to face the world—starting with the assault of a nasty spate of February weather. Opening one eye, she saw what she knew by scent and habit would be there: a steaming bowl of *café au lait* on her bedside table placed there by Laurent who of course had been up for hours.

The aroma of the coffee did its work and she pushed herself up to a sitting position and reached for the bowl. Knowing how she enjoyed the view first thing in the morning—and how the creeping sunlight would help wake her—Laurent had pulled back the drapes in the bedroom.

Through the steam rising from the bowl she could see the outline of the antique Juliette balcony outside the window and the dramatic sweep of the vineyard beyond. She took a sip of her coffee, relishing its rich flavor as well as the warmth of her bed. From this distance the pruned vines were just black stumps sticking out of the ground. After seven years and seven harvests, Maggie knew there was life in what looked like a field of devastation. There was in fact the beginning of next August's harvest although its merit would depend on sunshine and the spring and summer rains.

Maggie could also see the distant truffle oaks and cypresses that framed the borders of the vineyard, and the rows of olive and fig trees leading from the back garden along a pebbled path to the vineyard.

"*Maman!*" a child's voice cried out. It was immediately followed by the low, rumble of Laurent's voice.

Maggie sighed. Her peace was coming to an end. Not that she didn't adore the moment when her children flung open her bedroom door and climbed onto the bed to greet her as they often did. But there was something about this morning that made Maggie want to linger.

Want to put off getting out of bed to face the day.

And she knew very well why.

She looked up as her bedroom door swung open. Laurent stood in the opening, their daughter Mila in his arms. His light brown hair hung to his shoulders. His eyes were dark, nearly pupilless. Maggie always found them sexy but a little disconcerting too because she could never read them. His eyes were a lot like Laurent, himself. Mysterious.

A big man, Laurent stood over six foot five, with broad shoulders and even edging toward his mid-forties carried not an ounce of fat. It always amazed Maggie how Laurent seemed to effortlessly manage that—especially since he was such an amazing cook.

"See?" Laurent said to the child as he stepped into the room. "*Maman* is alive and well. Now it is time for everyone to get dressed." He raised an eyebrow at Maggie to underscore his statement.

"I'm up. I'm up," Maggie said, pushing back the warm covers. "Race you downstairs for pancakes?"

The child kicked her feet to be let down. Laurent put her down and Mila quickly disappeared out the door. Maggie's little dog Petit-Four jumped out of her dog bed and followed the child downstairs.

"Is everybody up?" Maggie asked as she put on her slippers. Her parents had come to France for Christmas and never left—unusual for them. Maggie's niece Nicole had spent three weeks with them at Domaine St-Buvard, Maggie and Laurent's *mas*, but had recently flown back to Atlanta to go skiing with school friends.

Nicole was seventeen now with no apparent memory of the traumatic first few years of her life. She excelled in school and was a loving cousin to Maggie's children Jemmy and Mila.

"Of course," Laurent said wryly as if to imply that only Maggie could still be asleep with so much noise going on in the house.

Maggie's friend Grace Van Sant and her ten-year old daughter Zouzou had gotten in late last night.

Maggie and Grace had been the best of friends when Maggie first came to France over nine years ago. But their friendship had taken a serious hit two years ago—one that Maggie was sure they would never come back from.

"Zouzou is a problem," Laurent said flatly. His comment surprised Maggie first because there were very few things that Laurent ever admitted were a problem for him, and secondly because all children everywhere routinely adored him. As gruff and bearish as he was—or perhaps *because* he was so gruff—children tended to gyrate toward him. And problem children? There was no such thing as far as Laurent was concerned.

"Seriously?" Maggie said. "You can tell that already? She's been here, what, eight hours and asleep for most of them?"

Laurent shrugged. As usual, his response was enigmatic. But if Laurent said Zouzou was a problem, that meant something.

Maggie sighed. "Are you going to be okay with her?" Maggie and Grace were scheduled to leave that afternoon for a five day retreat at a ski resort in Grenoble where they would try to work out their problems and find their way back to a friendship again. The plan was for Zouzou to stay at Domaine St-Buvard with Laurent.

Laurent only snorted.

"What is it with Grace and children?" Maggie said with annoyance as she slipped into her robe. "First Taylor and now Zouzou."

Grace's oldest child Taylor had always been a trial but Zouzou had been the cheerier and more docile of the two. Any way you looked at it, Maggie thought, it looked like Grace had taken a perfectly sweet kid and somehow turned Zouzou into a horror show just like her big sister.

Or maybe Maggie was just feeling down on Grace these days.

Eighteen months ago Grace had been living with Maggie and Laurent while the rest of Grace's life was falling apart around her. *Correction*, Maggie thought—*while Grace was singlehandedly dismantling her life around her*. Grace had gone on a spending spree with money she didn't have for a business that gave every sign of failing from the beginning, while ignoring both her daughters and leaving the care of them to Laurent and Maggie or anybody else who'd take them.

In the end Grace's bad judgment had led to Mila's being abducted at a public fête providing Maggie with the worst nine hours of her life.

So, yes. Grace had a long way to go to prove she was a friend to Maggie.

"People don't change," Maggie said.

"I think what we have been saying is the exact opposite of that," Laurent said.

"Yes, well, I'm talking about Grace now," Maggie said. "Not Zouzou."

"Get dressed, *chérie*," Laurent said ominously as he turned to leave. "And dress warmly. It is cold inside and out today."

2

WASH, RINSE, REPEAT

Laurent was right about Zouzou.

Maggie was standing next to her mother Elspeth Newberry in the kitchen and watched as the truculent preteen sat apart from the group, her iPad in her hands, a permanent scowl on her face. Zouzou was short for her age with long blonde hair down her back. She had a heart-shaped face and bow lips with lively blue eyes. She had been chubby the last time Maggie had seen her. She was bordering on fat now.

Was she stress eating? Was it genetic? Grace was willow slim and Taylor was as skinny as a wire. It was true Zouzou's biological father had not been skinny but nothing like this.

"Are you going to be all right, darling?" Elspeth asked her.

Maggie looked at her mother in surprise.

"Why wouldn't I be?"

Ever since she'd arrived at Domaine St-Buvard five weeks ago Maggie's mother had hinted at how tired she was and how busy and overwhelmed her schedule was given all of Nicole's school activities and Elspeth's own daily round of bridge parties and country club luncheons with friends.

And then of course there was Maggie's father. John Newberry, on the surface, often appeared to be his old jolly self during the holidays—only half listening to what anyone said and responding to even serious inquiries with a laugh and a good natured shrug. But there had been a few instances of temper that Maggie had never seen from him before.

And then there was his memory. Not just short term. There were moments when he would look at the children and Maggie would swear he wasn't sure who they were.

Was that what was bothering her mother?

Has there been a diagnosis that she's trying to bring herself to tell me about?

Maggie knew her parents had had a rough last couple of years, mostly because of Maggie's older brother Ben. Their granddaughter Nicole who they were raising had been nothing but a joy to them but Nicole would be going away to college soon.

"You just seem a little tense, is all," Elspeth said and looked away.

I could say the same of you, Maggie thought. But she'd long since given up trying to get her mother to tell her what was on her mind before she was ready. Elspeth was a lot like Laurent in that way.

"Laurent's concerned about Zouzou," Maggie said.

"Zouzou is fine and Laurent knows it," Elspeth said. "It's you he's worried about."

Maggie nearly laughed. "That's ridiculous. *He's* the one on the front lines this week. I'm going on *vacation.* "

"*Are* you, darling?" Elspeth said, raising an eyebrow before glancing across the room where Grace sat with a cup of coffee.

Except for a brief greeting last night when Grace and Zouzou got in, Maggie hadn't said much to Grace. She figured they'd have plenty of time to hash all that out during their five days at the ski resort—although Maggie was really hoping to get some skiing in. She hadn't skied in years and she'd so loved it when she was in college and used to make the weekend jaunts up to Sugar Mountain in North Carolina from Atlanta.

"I'm fine," Maggie said firmly. "Danielle will come over if you need anything and otherwise Laurent has everything under control."

"As he always does."

"That's right. As he always does. You are acting so strange," Maggie said with exasperation. She looked around the room. Laurent had finished making the last plate of pancakes and was handing them out to Jemmy and Maggie's father. Her father smiled dotingly at his grandson.

"We'll be fine here," her mother said, following Maggie's eye to where John Newberry sat next to Jemmy. "Your father comes alive when he's with Jemmy."

Maggie was startled to hear her mother say that although she knew it was true. *Is it because of the whole mess with Ben?* Was her father so discouraged by all that had happened with his only son that he'd jumped a generation to pin all his hopes and dreams on the next one?

All through the holidays, her father had spent much more time with Jemmy than with Mila. It was true her father was a man's man—down to the hunting dogs, the cigars, the glass of bourbon in the library at night and the expectation that the women in his life would honor him and his decisions no matter how misguided they might be.

The quintessential Southern gent, Maggie thought as she watched her father. She'd always loved that about him.

But she didn't want it for her son.

"Your father thinks Jemmy will make an amazing lawyer some day," Elspeth said. "When you move back to the US."

And there it was.

Maggie bit her lip to ensure she didn't over react. This wasn't the first time this visit that her mother had mentioned how she hoped Maggie and Laurent would move back to the States.

Maggie didn't know which she was more upset about—the fact that her parents were already pushing their own preferences for Jemmy's future—or that they believed Maggie would come back to the US.

But now was not the time to respond.

"Laurent hopes Jemmy will become a *vigneron* like him," Maggie said and then cursed the fact that she'd responded in spite of her best intentions.

"Oh, not seriously, surely?" Elspeth said. "Jemmy is so smart."

Are you saying Laurent isn't? But this time Maggie managed not to say it outloud.

Laurent looked over at Maggie and frowned. She knew he couldn't hear their conversation from where he stood—no matter how acute his hearing was—but he seemed to be able to tell things from the vibrations in the air.

She forced herself to smile at him as if to say *No problem. All is well.*

He probably can read the lie in that too, she thought

"After all, our children are who they will be," Elspeth said, blithely continuing the conversation. "Remember that, darling. You and Laurent are just along for the ride."

"Yep," Maggie said, biting her lip hard. "Good to know."

An hour later, Maggie stood by the taxi parked in the front drive of Domaine St-Buvard. Laurent stood beside her, a leather Louis Vuitton train case on the ground in front of them.

Grace was having a last minute tête-a-tête with Zouzou on the front steps of the house. Their words were muted but the intense expressions on both their faces left little doubt that a warning was being issued and *not* received well at all.

"Promise me you won't wallop her while we're gone," Maggie said to him, only half joking.

"I make no promises."

Maggie shivered and Laurent automatically put an arm around her. It was cold with a light dusting of snow already on the ground. The strong scent of roasting grapevines filled the air. Laurent had been pruning and burning the vinestocks already this morning. She could smell the woodsmoke in his jacket as she leaned into him.

For a moment, she was sorry he wasn't going with her. It had been ages since the two of them had gotten away—before Mila was born four years ago.

She looked up at the façade of their home. Sometimes she indulged herself by trying to remember how it felt to see Domaine St-Buvard for the first time. How seeing it nine years ago had filled her with hope and longing and delight. And a little fear.

A large stone terrace splayed out from the front door in three stepped tiers to the curving gravel drive. Oleander and ivy clustered against the fieldstone walls of the house in thick tangles of dark green. A black wrought-iron railing framed the second-story balcony that jutted out over the front door. The three sets of bedroom windows on the second floor were tall and mullioned and framed with bright blue shutters.

As a country *mas*, the house was bigger and older than most in the area. After years of renovations and gradual design additions it was now a stylish and comfortable family home for the family of four.

"You think this is a bad idea, don't you?" she said. "Me and Grace going off like this."

"*Pas du tout*," he said with a shrug.

Which meant, in Laurent-speak, *very probably yes*.

Maggie blew lightly on her hands and stamped her feet. A thick band of clouds overhead had sunk the front terrace steps into deep shadow and she felt the chill.

As Grace turned away from Zouzou, who turned and stomped into the house, pushing past Jemmy and Mila as they came outside, Maggie squeezed Laurent's hand. He leaned over and kissed her.

"Keep your cellphone on," he said.

"You're one to talk."

Laurent was notorious for forgetting to carry his phone or letting the battery die.

Jemmy and Mila ran over to hug Maggie goodbye. She kissed them both.

"Be good for Papa, okay?" Maggie said, smoothing down Jemmy's wild hair, so very like what Maggie imagined Laurent's must have looked like as a boy. The two were so similar in so many ways. Just maybe not in the important ones?

"Of course," Jemmy said. He'd taken to speaking only English since his grandparents had arrived—another point of contention, Maggie knew, with Laurent. Her ears still rang with Laurent's comment last night after dinner when her father had announced how proud he would be when Jemmy joined his Uncle Ben's old law firm.

"I would rather he join the flic than become un avocat," Laurent had said as he and Maggie got ready for bed last night. *I'd rather he be a cop than a lawyer.* And in light of Laurent's past life as a criminal on the *Côte d'Azur, that* spoke volumes as to how much he did *not* want his son to take the law as his vocation.

Maggie hugged both children again and gave Laurent one last kiss before getting into the taxi beside Grace.

Grace was wearing a Burberry quilted parka that hugged her every curve that Maggie knew couldn't have cost less than a thousand US dollars. Maggie wasn't sure how Grace was doing for money these days but clearly she wasn't shopping the sales bin at Macy's.

"Are you ready for this?" Grace asked lightly as she smoothed the nonexistent creases from her coal black wool slacks.

"Of course," Maggie said, waving to her family as the car drove away. "Why wouldn't I be?"

3

BLOWING SMOKE

Laurent watched the taxi creep down the long curving drive of Domaine St-Buvard. The snow had turned into brown sludge that now clumped down the center of the gravel drive.

When Laurent had inherited the *mas* and surrounding hectares of vineyard from his Uncle Nicolas nine years ago he'd merely hoped that some day he might be able to bring the ancient vineyard back. At the time he'd wanted only to be able to produce a simple *vin de pays*. Something he could put the Dernier name on. Maybe pass on to his children.

At the thought of Jemmy, Laurent turned toward the house.

Towering Italian cypress trees and Tatarian dogwoods flanked the massive front door. In summer hollyhocks would push out in a riot of bushes by the front steps. But now there was just the stone lion—its head bowed, one ear chipped as it had been for a century—standing guard on the stone threshold that led into Domaine St-Buvard.

"She'll be fine, Laurent," his mother-in-law Elspeth said to him as he stepped into the ancient *mas*. She was a beautiful woman, Elspeth. Laurent had no doubt that her lifelong wealth had helped preserve the affect. But he had to admit she was essentially good-humored. Born that way if he had to guess.

"I am not worried about Maggie," he said, his full lips curving into a smile. "Only what there is for dinner tonight."

"Well, I can hardly believe that," Elspeth said. "I'm sure you have everything in the kitchen under control."

Laurent was known for many things in the family but his ability *dans la cuisine* was the most prominent.

"Where are the children?" he asked as he scanned the foyer and hall leading to the living room.

"I am here, Papa!" Little Mila piped up from the kitchen. "Waiting for you!"

Laurent smiled at the sound of his daughter's voice. If someone had told him a decade ago that he would receive an immediate jolt of warmth and joy in response to a little girl's voice, he would simply not have believed it.

"I believe they are all waiting for you," Elspeth said as she moved ahead of him into the kitchen.

The kitchen was painted a pale ochre yellow with sporadic persimmon touches. The window over the sink was wide and faced the front driveway. Most days it brought in the Mediterranean sun that infused the kitchen with a yellow glow. The floors were terracotta and featured a matching backsplash. Maggie would have preferred something a little more feminine— perhaps something with hand-painted flowers—but this was Laurent's space and it was designed for utilitarian use. The resulting look was clean, airy, and masculine.

As Laurent entered the kitchen he saw their neighbor Danielle Alexandre sitting at the counter with a cup of coffee before her. She was flanked by both Mila and Jemmy. In the absence of their American grandparents who normally resided in Atlanta, Danielle and her husband Jean-Luc had taken up the challenge of being acting grandparents to the children.

"*Bonjour*, Laurent," Danielle said. Her eyes looked hollow and her face gaunt. The chemotherapy had taken its toll on her but all agreed it was for the best. She was in remission now. As Laurent came into the room and kissed her on both cheeks, he immediately sensed that there was something wrong.

"I did not want to distract from your goodbyes," Danielle said, smiling wanly. Her brown hair heavily streaked with grey was twisted into an attractive but unfashionable bun at the nape of her neck "So I came in the back."

"I saw her first, Papa!" Mila said excitedly. Mila was a beautiful child, blonde with dark blue eyes and a rosebud mouth. Except for Maggie's dark hair, Laurent always thought Mila looked like her mother.

"Did you, *ma petite*?" Laurent said, cupping the child's cheek lightly before moving into the center of his kitchen. He had been in the process of making a *tagine* for lunch and went to his mortar and pestle to begin creating the spice mixture he'd use in the African dish.

Elspeth sat down next to Danielle. A large potted lavender plant perched on the breakfast counter.

"Danielle was telling me that Jean-Luc isn't feeling well," Elspeth said, her eyes too bright as she spoke.

"*Ah oui?*" Laurent said noncommittally as he shook out equal amounts of ginger and cardamom into the heavy marble bowl.

"It is nothing," Danielle said. "The flu I'm sure."

"Jemmy," Laurent said, "go find Zouzou and tell her to come down."

"She wants to be alone," Jemmy said.

Laurent turned and glanced at him, one eyebrow shooting high into his brown fringe. Jemmy got down from his stool with a sigh and went to walk upstairs to the bedrooms.

From where Laurent stood he could see through the main salon past the back terrace and to the sweeping fields of his vineyard.

The vineyard was cut by two narrow dirt and gravel roads into quadrants. Last year's harvest had been a good one, easily the best of all seven so far. But the spring rains had bleached the sweetness from the grapes and the Mistral had destroyed nearly a quarter of the vines—whisking them away back to Morocco or wherever the hell the demon winds came from.

Next year will be better, Laurent thought and then grimaced at the thought.

"Papa? Can I cut some rosemary sprigs from the *potager*?" Mila said, jumping down from her stool and snatching up the shears from a hook by the stove. Laurent's *potager* was through the dining room and off the back terrace.

"You must not run with those," he remarked to the child before glancing at the two older women at the counter. "You will stay for lunch, Danielle?" he asked.

"*Mais non*, Laurent. *Merci*," Danielle said. "I just came by to say hello."

And to tell me about Jean-Luc.

"Tell Jean-Luc I will come by later," he said as he turned back to his stove. Through the window over the sink he caught a glimpse of movement in the front drive and saw that it was Zouzou. The child moved sluggishly, trudging up the drive and then turning and walking back down. Was she doing it for exercise?

Jemmy returned to the kitchen. "I couldn't find her. What do you want me to do now?"

"Supervise your sister," Laurent said without taking his eyes off Zouzou. What was the girl doing?

As Danielle got up to leave, his cellphone rang

"I will tell Jean-Luc you will come," she said to Laurent as she and Elspeth moved through the salon and out the back terrace door.

"*D'accord*," Laurent said and then accepted the call.

"I have not yet decided," he said curtly into the phone and then hung up.

His emotions juddered through him as he held the phone in his hand and waited for his feelings to settle. He could see Zouzou again and he watched her as she went to the end of the drive where it connected with the road that led to the village.

Laurent's eyes were good. Very good. But he didn't need to see that well to recognize the motions of what Zouzou was doing as she pulled something out of her coat pocket and stuffed it into her mouth.

4

SO FAR APART

The temperature had fallen rapidly with the late afternoon by the time Maggie and Grace's taxi arrived at the front door of the *Chalet Savoir Faire*. The fog that had accompanied their drive from the *Gare de Grenoble* was thinner now having evolved into faint wisps that hovered close to the cobblestone pavement in front of the ski chalet.

As Grace got out of the taxicab the brief arctic bite of breeze gave her a rush of memory of happier times. She pushed the memories of Kitzbuhl and St-Moritz from her mind. Those places were from a time long ago.

A time when I had money and a family.

She immediately performed a mental exercise that her therapist Ruth back in Atlanta had taught her called thought-stopping. Whenever Grace found herself thinking of how she'd sabotaged her life—her friendships, her relationships with her children, not to mention her marriage to Windsor—she would mentally pinch herself and say "ouch" as softly as possible to bring it to her attention.

You manage what you monitor, Ruth would say and, as tiresome and ultimately annoying as Grace always found the woman, she knew she was right.

Maggie hadn't said three words on the train ride to the village. That was so unlike Maggie that Grace figured it had to be deliberate.

Or who knows? Maybe Maggie really doesn't have anything to say to me.

A prick of melancholy pierced Grace at the thought and she pinched herself. It didn't help to go there. She'd learned that if nothing else.

"Ouch," she murmured.

"Did you say something?" Maggie asked politely, looking around as if to find the reason for Grace's utterance.

"Not really, darling," Grace said with a smile. "Just excited about our retreat."

She could see a wince of emotion flit across Maggie's face. Grace had had to seriously talk her into this trip and she knew it was only the prospect of being able to ski that ultimately had gotten Maggie on board.

Maggie doesn't want to be friends again.

Grace swallowed hard and pushed the thought away, mentally pinching herself for all she was worth.

Don't think that. It doesn't help.

This time she voiced the *ouch* only in her mind.

As she stepped out of the taxi, Maggie observed the front of the ski lodge. It was made of brick and stone—unusual for the area— and featured a small bay window showcasing a pair of posed mannequins wearing colorful ski resort clothing. Each mannequin was leaning on a pair of skis, their pom-pom knit hats perched jauntily on their heads to give an almost macabre sense of premonition to the place.

While the chalet was clearly very old, it did appear as if it had been recently renovated, which Maggie could tell from the tacked-on modern additions on either side. But the main section of the building—ancient soot-stained yellow brick—looked as if dated back to the time of the French Revolution. One look at its ancient beams and the elaborately carved front lintel that hung over the front door made Maggie believe that guess was entirely possible.

As long as they had Wi-Fi and decent coffee—and what resort mountain chalet didn't?—it was perfectly fine as far as Maggie was concerned. A fissure of pleasurable spite stung her when she thought how differently Grace must be viewing all of this.

Instantly, Maggie scolded herself. Envisioning—and then reveling—in the thought of Grace's reaction to staying at a one-star hotel was beneath her.

Satisfying, but beneath her.

Once through the front door Maggie didn't wait for the hand-some-if-aging bellhop or Grace for that matter—but strode purposefully to the front desk.

It had freshly snowed in Grenoble that morning but her phone's weather app had accurately predicted the sun would be out all afternoon—making for amazing weather for downhill. Clear, cold, very little wind. She only hoped the next five days would be as nice.

Grace trailed behind Maggie as she stood at the registration desk and hit the front desk bell. The lobby was full of people dressed for the slopes or for travel. It had been Maggie's idea to book the trip for after the weekend so that they might take advantage of lower rates and fewer people. If even only half the people in the lobby were leaving, it bode well for having a pleasant uncrowded experience on the slopes.

"*Oui*, Madame?" A woman wearing the nametag *Alys Chaix* hurried around the counter. In her early thirties, she had curly chestnut-colored hair that framed large brown eyes and the bowed lips of a Botticelli angel. She brought with her a wafting of floral fragrance. Maggie was instantly reminded of her grandmother.

"Welcome to *Chalet Savoir Faire*," the concierge said.

"*Merci*," Maggie said. "We have two rooms reserved through February 27."

"Great minds," a male voice in an English accent bellowed over Maggie's shoulder. She turned to see a man with ruddy cheeks and a bulbous nose standing behind Grace. He grinned at Maggie. "I'm staying through the twenty-seventh as well."

Before Maggie could respond, Grace turned to address the man.

"How nice for you," she said sweetly.

That was classic Grace. Polite on the surface but a slow burn when you thought about it. It was clear that the guy hadn't really looked at Grace—which he definitely did now—because he reacted the way most mortal men did when they laid eyes on a goddess incarnate.

Grace was a beauty and there was no mistake about that. She was Grace Kelly with all the poise and style you'd expect from a mythical creature.

In Grace's case however, Maggie knew exactly how much myth was involved.

"I...I...well, I..." the man stuttered as he gazed dumbfounded at Grace.

Grace turned from him and gave Maggie a small conspiratorial smile and for just a moment Maggie was tempted to return the smile. But she didn't. She turned back to the concierge who was pushing two room keys across the counter at her.

"The Wi-Fi code is on the back of the resort brochure," Madame Chaix said with a smile and then looked past Maggie and Grace at the Englishman. "Monsieur?"

Maggie stepped away from the desk and spotted the bellhop standing with their luggage. He looked too old to be a proper bellhop but he was still quite handsome. His nametag read *Max*

Fountainbleu. Behind him was a table with a series of stacked glossy brochures and a sign that read in English "Ski Lesson Signup." A picture of Max from years earlier was on the sign.

"I guess he does double duty," Grace commented as she and Maggie approached the man and handed him their room keys.

Before they reached the stairs, Maggie saw a set of French doors that opened onto what looked to be the dining room. She tapped Max on the shoulder to indicate he should wait.

"I just want to see the view from here," Maggie said to Grace. "TripAdvisor said it was magnificent."

"Of course, darling," Grace said as the two stepped into the dining room.

The entrance to the dining room featured an open entryway with a vaulted ceiling supported on rows of squat ornate pillars and a large crystal chandelier. A massive display window immediately afforded a dramatic view of Peak Etendard—the major summit of the French Alps' Grandes Rousses—soaring three thousand meters above sea level.

As Maggie gazed at the stunning view, she felt a ping of excitement race through her at the thought of skiing the mountain tomorrow.

Branching off from the dining room was a hallway that opened up on the other side of the kitchen. From where they stood Maggie could see a massive aquarium built into the wall that made up nearly one whole side of the hall wall.

It occurred to Maggie that a narrow passageway en route to the restrooms was an odd place to put such an enormous fish tank. While it was true that guests would be able to see the pretty fish on their way to and from the restrooms, the hall was too narrow to afford more than an extremely truncated view.

Scanning the rest of the dining room, Maggie was surprised to see that there were still people eating. It was late afternoon and she would have expected lunch to be long over. A tall man wearing a toque and chef's jacket stood next to a table positioned closest to the window and the view of the mountain. A young Indian couple sat at the table. The Indian man was not happy.

The chef leaned over the young Indian man to say a few words that Maggie couldn't hear which prompted the young man to fling down his napkin and jump to his feet.

"I say! That is total rubbish! I'll have the management know immediately, you racist cretin!" the young Indian man said hotly, his face shoved close to the chef's.

"*Pardonez-moi,*" Max said politely and pushed past Grace and Maggie. He strode to the table and spoke to the chef in a low voice. Maggie saw the chef turn on Max as if he would transfer his ire to *him* but when he saw that he was being observed by her and Grace his face flushed and he stormed out of the room.

Max quickly delivered his apologies to the young couple and then rejoined Grace and Maggie. He collected their bags and carried them upstairs to the first two rooms on the second floor. He set the bags down on the carpet to manage the keys. As he did, the door to the room across the hall opened and a man in his mid-forties stepped out followed by a woman of about the same age with a thin, sharp-boned face and a severe pixie cut.

"*Attends,* Max!" the man called out. "Glad we caught you! Can you fit us in for a lesson tomorrow morning, say about ten?"

Max nodded. "*Oui,* Monsieur Toureille," he said. "No problem." He nodded at the woman. "Madame Toureille."

At his words the couple giggled and, holding hands, retreated down the hall toward the stairs.

"If they're married to each other," Grace said, "I'm Katy Perry."

Max opened the door to Maggie's room but she noticed a sly smile from him at Grace's words.

So he understands English, Maggie thought. *Good to know.*

"I take it you are the ski instructor?" Maggie asked, knowing perfectly well he was.

"If you are interested in lessons," he said, "I should warn you that weather conditions are thought to be worsening."

Maggie pressed her lips together.

"Do you mean there won't be enough snow?" she asked. "Or that high temps are coming to melt the snow on the ground?"

He shook his head. "A front is coming through."

"So that would mean *more* snow, wouldn't it?" Grace asked helpfully.

"*Oui*, Madame. *Too* much snow. Very dangerous conditions."

Maggie sighed, tipped him and went into her room tossing a cavalier, "see you in the dining room" over her shoulder to Grace who stood expectantly in the hallway.

Maggie closed her door.

Lisa settled into the worn but grand luxury of the velvet banquette bench and smiled at Serge as he made his way to the hotel bar for their midday drinkies. The moment his back was turned, she relaxed her smile muscles, stifling a sigh when she did.

Being a tireless sex goddess was exhausting, she thought. Especially at forty. *No wonder women marry*, she thought. *No one can keep this charade up twenty-four seven.*

As she waited for Serge to return with their drinks she glanced around the chalet's lobby.

Shabby chic, indeed. A tired looking grouping of a dozen or so armchairs upholstered in the matching burgundy brocade of the wallpaper faced the banquette where she sat, a scuffed wooden coffee table in front of her. The lobby looked like it had come straight out of the pages of some post-war novella. How had this place ever managed to get recommended on any of the online travel sites by anyone with any kind of taste or style?

And she'd so been looking forward to this week! Serge had

insisted on keeping the name of the resort a secret—one of his little surprises he'd said—but Lisa was sure it was to prevent her from looking it up online.

After weeks of hushed phone conversations and sexy texts back and forth from Brighton to Paris, this week was all Lisa had been able to think of. She shook herself out of her negative thoughts.

I'm with Serge and that's all that matters. Not the lobby or how well the hotel is rated.

She watched the ski instructor as he leaned on the registration counter to talk to the pretty concierge. The man's shoes were scuffed, his clothes worn and dated.

Lisa shifted uncomfortably on the banquette and realized there was a spring loose that was poking her from within the upholstery.

Somehow, in her fantasies about this week, everything had been a bit different.

She heard Serge laughing from the bar and she scolded herself again, reminding herself what this week was all about.

What difference did it make if the place was a shambles? They had each other. The last two nights had been beyond anything Lisa could have imagined. Serge only wanted to look into her eyes and hear every single detail about what made her tick. He wanted to hear about who she was, her thoughts, her dreams—and how he might fit into them.

She shivered with pleasure and then glanced at her watch with a sudden anxiety that she just as quickly quashed when she saw what time it was. She wouldn't need another injection for at least another hour. As long as Serge didn't insist on a pre-dinner walk, she would have plenty of opportunity to slip away to the ladies loo and deal with it without him knowing a thing.

Another burst of laughter came to her from the bar—this time female—that made Lisa think of the incident in the hallway just a few moments ago.

The two American women had glanced at her when she and Serge had come out of their shared room.

Not just glanced but *judged*.

Lisa had tried to laugh it off—had even succeeded in snickering with Serge once they were out of earshot, after all, what were the poor creatures doing here alone without lovers or husbands? *Pathétique*, as Serge had said. But all the same something unpleasant had struck Lisa when she'd exchanged glances with the women.

Especially the beautiful blonde one. She'd regarded Lisa with an arched eyebrow and a knowing, condescending smile...as if she knew that Lisa wasn't married to Serge, and that sharing a room with a handsome Frenchman was something any common person could do.

How is it possible that so much can be conveyed by one two-second glance?

But Lisa knew how. After all, wasn't that what she did for a living? Turning nothing into drama and tension?

Maybe Mum was right. Perhaps she'd had her head stuck too long in a book. She wouldn't be at all surprised to discover that that was true. But didn't this week with Serge in the French Alps disprove that?

It's not a fantasy when you wake up each morning to a French lover who'd rather have you for breakfast than his morning croissant.

Lisa picked up her purse next to her on the velvet-tufted bench and quickly hunted up a notepad and pen from inside.

It's not a fantasy when you wake up each morning to a French lover who'd rather have you than his morning croissant.

Some lines were just too good to waste.

5

A SEA CHANGE

The drive to Jean-Luc's house that afternoon was a quiet one. Zouzou sat in the passenger seat of Laurent's Renault gnawing her nails and staring glumly out the window at the bleak winter scape. Normally this area of Provence received very little snow and Jemmy and Mila had been delighted with the surprise snowfall. Although it hadn't snowed now in several days, neither had the temperature risen high enough to melt off what there was from the ditches and stone bridges that surrounded the area of Domaine St-Buvard.

"Why do you feel a need to snack when I have made you breakfast?" Laurent asked abruptly. Regardless of the fact that he once made his living as a con artist—misrepresenting himself on every level—he found that with children, the best way to find out what you wanted was often the most direct way. Although Laurent had no experience with teenagers, he had to assume they were not that different.

After all, they were still basically children.

Zouzou didn't answer him. In Laurent's experience, unless they were afraid, all children loved to talk. Typically, it was getting them to stop talking that was the trick.

"Z?" he prompted. He had called her this since she was very small. As *Oncle* Laurent's pet name for her it used to always delight her then.

Still there was no response from her.

Debating whether to pull the car over and insist she answer him or ignore the failed attempt at communication, Laurent frowned and watched the girl. She did in fact have a pretty face. Unlike her older sister Taylor who was dark haired with angular features, Zouzou took after her beautiful mother. Was the weight gain genetic? Or the result of unhappiness? Laurent certainly was in no position to know—even if he had all winter to study Zouzou. He shook off his inclination to fix what was wrong with the child.

Best to just demand she respect me while she's in my house and look forward to seeing the back of her when it was time.

But that didn't feel right either.

Opting to let her have her silence—he would find another route to get the answers he wanted—Laurent turned on the car radio and drove the rest of the way to Jean-Luc's house without attempting to engage her again.

Jean's Luc's house was typical of the old farmhouses in the area. Built of stone in the 1700s, it featured chipped blue shutters and terra cotta roofing and stood at the end of a long winding gravel drive. There were few times when Laurent drove to Jean-Luc's house that he didn't remember the first time he'd ever seen it. Years ago, with Maggie beside him, they'd come upon Jean-Luc with two of his hounds as he walked along the driveway before he surprised them both by jumping into the car and directing them to the top of the hill where the house sat.

Today Laurent parked behind Jean-Luc's old Citroen and handed the plastic container of left over *tagine* to Zouzou. A dog ran barking from around the house and jumped up on Zouzou as she got out of the car. Laurent rebuked him quickly but he thought he saw a glimmer of a smile on Zouzou's face as the dog continued to lick her hands and nudge her in greeting.

"*Bonjour*, Laurent, Zouzou!" Danielle sang out from the front door where she suddenly appeared. "Come in before you freeze!"

The interior of the house, unlike Maggie and Laurent's *mas*, was austere. When she married and moved in with Jean-Luc Danielle had added rag rugs to the worn wooden and tile floors and hung local artists' work on the stone washed walls. But except for the kitchen which was clearly Danielle's domain, the rest of the house was sparse—evidence of the decades of bachelor days when Jean-Luc had lived there alone.

Danielle ushered them both inside to a small room off the kitchen where a large Franklin stove sat in the corner warming the room. Jean-Luc hunched on a couch near the stove, a rug across his lap.

In his late sixties but looking older, Jean-Luc had grey hair with a thin, sharp-boned face and shrewd blue eyes. From the beginning Laurent had always known Jean-Luc as a crafty old fellow with many different agendas—mostly having to do with Laurent's land which decades earlier had been owned by Jean-Luc's family. It had taken Laurent years to fully trust Jean-Luc. And now he considered him, if not quite a father figure, then a beloved uncle.

"*Bonjour*, Jean-Luc," Laurent said shaking hands with the man and sitting next to him. "How are you then, eh?"

Jean-Luc shrugged. "As you see."

Danielle took the container of *tagine* from Zouzou. "*Chérie*, will you help me in the *cuisine*?"

Zouzou followed Danielle into the kitchen.

"Coffee and cake will be out in a minute," Danielle called to the men over her shoulder.

Laurent warmed his hands by the fire before turning to Jean-Luc. "Well?" he said.

Jean-Luc shook his head. "It's not a secret, Laurent."

"What is not a secret?"

"My health."

"Danielle said you have a flu bug."

"A flu bug that has lasted six months."

Laurent had to admit that Jean-Luc had begged off the usual tasks and get-togethers more often than not in the last few months. Laurent had been so busy with the wine business he hadn't noticed at the time. Both he and Jean-Luc, along with two others, had operated their vineyards under an alternating proprietorship that allowed them all to label their wines as produced and bottled by themselves.

But in the last two years, Laurent had decided to buy his own equipment and go it alone—with Jean-Luc of course. As that inevitably created more hands-on effort, without the help of co-op or partner vintners Laurent had necessarily taken over most of the work for both vineyards himself.

Jean-Luc picked up his steaming mug of coffee, his eyes narrowing on Laurent's face.

"Danielle and I are thinking of moving to Nice."

Laurent felt a sudden tingling in his core at Jean-Luc's words. This he had not expected.

Laurent prided himself on never deliberately giving away an emotion or intention but he had to force himself not to react at Jean-Luc's words. Although as soon as Jean-Luc said them Laurent found himself wondering why he was surprised. Clearly, they'd been heading this way for a long time now.

"Danielle's cancer—" Laurent began.

"This isn't about Danielle," Jean-Luc said. "Her cancer is in remission. This is about enjoying the sun in my old age."

"Retiring."

"If you like that word better." Jean-Luc shrugged.

"But you enjoy the vineyards, do you not? The different seasons? The rewards?" He wanted to say, *and your almost-grand-children? St-Buvard? Your neighbors and friends?*

"I have enjoyed it less and less with each passing year," Jean-Luc said. "You know yourself that you do most of the work. Let me sell my vineyard to you. I'll give you a fair price. You'll double the size of Domaine St-Buvard."

They sat quietly for a moment. The sounds from the kitchen filtered in to them. Danielle's voice was light and cheerful with the muffled clatter of cake plates and cups and saucers underneath it but Zouzou was speaking too. Somehow, Danielle was managing to do with the girl what Laurent couldn't.

"Your family has owned land in St-Buvard for two hundred years," Laurent said softly.

"Probably time to let someone else have a shot at it."

Laurent turned to look at him. Marrying late, Jean-Luc would leave no heirs to his land—or his name. His older brother Patrick had been a decorated Resistance fighter in the last war. Jean-Luc had dined well for many decades on the wartime heroics of his brother. Dead now for many years, Patrick had been accused of murdering an English couple and their children on the very doorstep of Laurent and Maggie's home, until Maggie had uncovered the truth sixty years later. Unfortunately it was too late for Jean-Luc's war hero brother. Patrick died in prison decades before Maggie and Laurent moved to Provence.

Danielle came into the room with a tray and set it down on a worn hassock in front of the stove.

"It sounds very serious in here," she said breezily as she poured coffees and began to cut thick crumbling wedges of vintner's grape cake.

"I told him our plans," Jean-Luc said.

"Oh?" Danielle looked at Laurent, her eyes probing. A typical French country woman, Danielle had moved to Provence thirty years earlier with her husband Eduard Morceau. It was an unhappy union, and when Eduard was forced to leave the area for a prison sentence, he granted Danielle an annullment, freeing her to marry the man she'd fallen in love with years earlier—Jean-Luc Alexandre. That was eight years ago but the two had been happy together ever since.

"Did you tell him about Eduard?" Danielle asked as she glanced over her shoulder to confirm that Zouzou was sitting at the kitchen counter eating her plate of cake and out of earshot.

Even though Zouzou was antisocial, Laurent had a suspicion she was sitting in the kitchen so no one could see how many pieces of cake she ate.

"What about Eduard?" he asked gruffly. Eduard had set fire to Laurent's vineyard the first year Laurent had moved to Buvard—and gone to prison for it.

"He's dead," Jean-Luc said, reaching for a piece of cake.

Laurent glanced at Danielle to see how she was taking Jean-Luc's statement but he could detect nothing in her eyes to suggest an unhappiness of any greater degree than if someone had told her one of the villagers had died.

"He was released from prison four years ago," Danielle said as she settled into a chair with her coffee. "I'm not sure if you knew that."

He did. There was very little that happened that might affect his world that Laurent did not make it his business to know. He nodded for her to continue.

"I understand he had a flat in Dijon," Danielle said. "He had a small pension."

Suddenly Laurent knew where this was going. Since Danielle and Eduard had their long marriage annulled instead of divorcing Eduard's house and vineyard would not go to Danielle. In the passing years, it had fallen into ruin—both the house and the grounds—which was generally seen by all as a great pity. At this stage, it would take a serious amount of investment to bring it back.

When Danielle and Jean-Luc exchanged a look, Laurent knew that Eduard had left his property to her.

He sighed and looked at his hands. If anything could make a person decide to give it all up, he thought, it would surely be the prospect of trying to renovate property as badly neglected as Eduard's.

"He left you the vineyard," he said.

"Yes," Danielle said.

"Would this be included in the property and lands you would want to sell?" he said to Jean-Luc. Eduard's land abutted Jean-Luc's, which abutted Laurent's.

"Of course," Jean-Luc said. "The point is to divest ourselves of land not hang on to some of it."

"And especially not Eduard's," Laurent pointed out. "The expense and work to bring it back would be immense."

"If you don't buy it, Laurent, we will sell it to someone else."

"Perhaps the new buyer will put up a Costco," Danielle said with a sly smile.

"Bite your tongue!" Jean-Luc said. "Never!"

"What do you care if you're moving to Nice?" Laurent said mildly.

"Oh, you're right," Jean-Luc said, his eyes brightening as he reached out to take Danielle's hand. "Go ahead then. Sell it to EuroDisney for all I care."

Danielle stood up to go into the kitchen. "Are you all right in here, *chérie*?" she called to Zouzou. "It's warmer in here by the fire."

Laurent didn't hear Zouzou's response although he assumed it was in the negative.

"I've heard in the village that you've made inquiries about possibly selling yourself," Jean-Luc said softly, reaching for another piece of cake.

When Laurent didn't answer, Jean-Luc said, "You love your land."

"I did. It's possible I will love it less without you."

"I don't believe that. My leaving is just an adjustment to be made. One more stage in a long life."

"Already I can see Mila and Jem will need to spend more time in Aix," Laurent said. "For school."

"Aix isn't that far away," Jean-Luc said. "Is there another reason you might want to sell?"

Laurent stood up. How to explain to him? How to put into words that it wasn't just the children or Maggie's mother's not-so-subtle hints to bring them all back to Atlanta or even Jean-Luc leaving? How to put into words that ever since Laurent had inherited the money from Aunt Delphine two years ago, the farm had felt so much less...essential than before?

Even after a backbreaking nine years the vineyard barely produced enough wine to support the family. And while it was true they didn't need the money—with his inheritance and Maggie's newsletter doing so well—it rankled Laurent to see his life's work reduced to the level and dignity of a hobby.

"Nice will be good for you and Danielle," he said finally. "I can see you now taking your daily walk down the *Promenade des Anglais* before your evening *apéro.*"

"*Moi aussi,*" Jean-Luc said, turning his gaze from Laurent to the fire. Laurent did not know what the old fellow saw in the flames but he was pretty sure it was not a summer evening on the *rue des Anglais.* So that was that, he thought. An era ending.

An hour later, Laurent and Zouzou were in the car headed back to Domaine St-Buvard. While Zouzou hadn't joined them in the other room, Laurent had been heartened to hear her talk with Danielle in the kitchen. By the time they left Jean-Luc and Danielle's driveway and reached the main road the weak winter sun was quickly disappearing behind a thick band of clouds. It was much colder too. The snow would never melt at this rate.

Laurent's mind was buzzing with the implications of his conversation with Jean-Luc, of buying Jean-Luc's property and also Eduard's which would create a significant landholding for Laurent. It was true that except for the initial work and cost to bring Eduard's vines back it was all good land for grapes.

But for what purpose?

"Did you enjoy your visit with Madame Alexandre?" Laurent asked distractedly.

Silence filled the car and Laurent turned to glance at the girl. Zouzou leaned against the car door, her head against the window, her eyes watching the dreary landscape outside.

"I require you to answer me when I speak to you," he said.

She turned her head to look at him, her eyes defiant, her lips pressed together in a firm line.

"*Bon*," he said, pulling the car over onto the verge, the tires scraping into the gravel and mud.

Zouzou put her hands on the dashboard, her eyes wide with concern.

"Get out," he said.

"What?" She looked out the window at the lonely road, the snow muddy and frozen over along the ditch. The late afternoon sun had fallen behind thick clouds and the line of trees that bordered the road.

Laurent leaned over, disconnected her seatbelt and threw open the passenger door. "Out," he said.

She looked at him her eyes rapidly blinking in shock. "You can't do this," she said but she slid out of her seat. Without answering, Laurent reached over to grab the passenger door, slammed it shut and drove away.

6

STRANGER ON THE SHORE

Outside Aishwarya's window the wind gusted up, driving a flurry of snow against her windowpane. She had a good view from her room of the gravel round-about drive and the highway that led to the more famous ski resorts of Valfréjus and Valloire. The rooms on the other side of the hall had the mountain view and she knew they cost more.

She turned away from the uninspiring view outside and fought down her disappointment. She tried to remember how excited she'd been when she knew they were coming to Grenoble for their honeymoon. *It's just a stupid view*, she thought. *It's certainly not what matters.*

She went to the armoire to select her outfit for dinner. Just the thought of dinner made her take in a quick breath at the memory of the incident this afternoon in the dining room.

Why must Raj make a scene every time?

They'd only been at *Chalet Savoir Faire* two nights and he'd found fault with someone or something every single moment of that time. Aishwarya glanced at her cellphone and saw that her dear *Baba* had called again. A shudder shifted through her.

She didn't have the energy at the moment to fake one more

happy conversation with her mother. *Better she should think I'm too busy being blissful on my honeymoon*, she thought with mounting bitterness. Quickly, she tamped down the feelings.

This is your honeymoon! There is no room for anger! Or disappointment! And definitely no criticism of your husband!

She spread out her nylon cardigan with matching shell on the bed. It wouldn't keep her warm but Raj had complained that she looked matronly wearing wools. She would bring a cashmere pashmina to dinner with her. Her eye fell on the crimson sari in her opened suitcase.

Raj hated anything from the old country and he was especially unmerciful about Indian dress but Aishwarya couldn't help but love the romance and pure elegance of the sari. Her mother had given her this one before her wedding. It was exquisitely woven, mostly of silk but also with panels of decorative linen. And the drape! The way it fell in soft folds over her shoulder always made Aishwarya feel like a princess when she put it on.

A beautiful Indian princess.

She sighed. She wasn't sure why she'd brought it. Raj had made it clear he didn't want to see her wearing it. Ever since she was a little girl Aishwarya had dreamed of her wedding day and a beautiful sari that looked very much like this had definitely been a part of those dreams. To imagine that she would marry an Indian—completely delighting her parents in the process—and that he would be hardworking, industrious and career minded such that they would then move into a brick row house and Aishwarya wouldn't have to work—all of that was a dream that had been too big for Aishwarya to imagine.

And yet it had happened. Mostly.

She stood in front of the mirror and held up the sari in front of her. The color was good for her. It made her dark hair appear more vibrant. She knew she wasn't pretty but she had other qualities. She had a good figure that she worked to keep taut with daily yoga and relentless treadmilling—as much as she detested both. And she ate as little as she could possibly manage.

Raj liked to eat and she was sure he would love her cooking once they were actually living together. Because of the arrangement, she and Raj had only met once briefly before their wedding day. She'd been assured that he was drawn to her demureness and reserve. And she had been fascinated by his courage and confidence.

One of Aishwarya's bridesmaids—Becky—had taken Aishwarya aside two weeks before the wedding and told her that Raj had an ugly reputation as a player. The conversation had been upsetting but not for the reason Becky thought. Raj's habits before he met her didn't matter to Aishwarya. What did matter to her was that Becky obviously wanted to upset her or maybe even get her to call off the wedding.

She'd replaced Becky in her wedding and felt like she'd already handled the first of what her mother had warned her would be many trials in a long and happy married life.

Grace gazed out the window of her hotel room. She had a good view of Peak Etendard but she hoped Maggie's view was even better. She'd been surprised to see how cold Maggie was capable of being to her but then it was very possible that Grace had yet again underestimated the gravity of her crimes.

If Maggie didn't want to be friends again, Grace had no doubt her reasons were perfectly valid. In fact, it was probably downright selfish on Grace's part—yet again—to go to the lengths she was going to in order to win Maggie back. After all, what was in it for Maggie? Had Grace really been that good a friend to her? Even back in the good old days?

She sighed and got up to unpack her bag, shaking out her Tory Burch wool slacks and matching jacket.

It had been a lucky break for Grace, however, that the weather might cooperate with her plans to make peace with Maggie. Grace was not a skier and the few words that Maggie had said to her on the train ride down had made it clear that Maggie intended to spend most of her time on the slopes.

Now she would be forced to spend time with Grace.

After she put her clothes away, Grace stepped out into the hall. She'd debated knocking on Maggie's door but Maggie had clearly said she wanted to get together tonight at dinner. Grace was determined to respect her wishes.

After all isn't that how I got in this fix in the first place? By pushing everyone else's desires aside for my own?

It was just as well. If Grace was going to create a miracle in the next five days she needed a plan. Successful outcomes didn't just happen. They were carefully orchestrated and executed. And like any good general, in order to set up a successful coup, she needed a good stratagem.

Step One was having a word with the resort chef to see if he might be talked into making one of Maggie's favorite dishes. One thing Grace knew about her friend was that she had a serious sweet tooth and found it difficult to be grumpy when biting into a creamy custard.

It wasn't much but sometimes the best results were based on the simplest of plans.

When Grace reached the lobby she noticed that it was nearly empty. All the people who had been there earlier when she and Maggie checked in must have been checking out.

There was an *aperitif* station set up in the corner of the lobby by the ancient grand piano. The chairs were worn but looked comfortable and there was a small fireplace in the corner that gave the setting a cozy effect. The Englishman who'd spoken to them earlier was sitting there with a drink in his hand. He looked startled when he saw Grace but when she acknowledged him with a nod, he blushed and grinned at her.

In a way the man reminded her of Garner. Oh, not so much in looks, but he was about the same age. There was an affect in older men, Grace noted, that showed itself around the eyes and the tilt of the head. It was as if to say, *I've seen it all and I still don't know what to make of it.*

And isn't that the very definition of wisdom?

In Grace's experience it was not something younger men tended to exude.

Leaving the lobby, she walked through the now empty dining room to the kitchen.

She glanced down the hall that held the impressive although oddly located aquarium and saw a small display alcove carved into the wall opposite the fish tank. The vertical glass display case held yet another mannequin. Like the ones in the lobby, this one was dressed in ski clothing too but it looked dated to Grace. If they hadn't been behind glass, she imagined the ski parkas would be coated with dust.

Turning back to the dining room, Grace noted that it was already dark outside even though it was barely five o'clock. The mountain visible through the window was more a looming shadow than something real. Grace shivered as she went through the set of double swinging doors that led to the kitchen.

The chef—the resort brochure said his name was Denis LeFleur—stood in the center of the kitchen. A young man stood with his back to the door where he was washing pots and pans. The chef stood with his hands on his hips and was talking in fast French to Max Fountainbleu who was now changed out of his bellhop uniform into slacks and a white shirt with an apron around his waist, clearly ready for his evening personae of dining room waiter.

The two men hadn't seen her yet and it gave Grace a moment to register the differences in them. Max was tall and handsome—if on the wrong side of fifty. He'd clearly been the handsome ski instructor most of his life until age had caught up with him. It was a shame, she thought. To go from the sexy ski instructor to bell hop/waiter must be a long way to fall.

The chef on the other hand, was younger, shorter and imminently unhappier. He was clean-shaven and wore a starched white chef's jacket. His face was flushed and tense and when he realized Grace was in the room, he literally jumped.

"*Bonjour,*" Grace said lightly, watching both men regard her in obvious guilt.

"May I help you, Madame?" Max asked, not looking Grace in the face but moving to put himself between her and the chef.

"*Merci,* Monsieur," Grace said, "but I was hoping to talk with Chef if possible."

"*Oui?*" LeFleur said abruptly, turning away from both of them and noisily opening a drawer of rattling silverware.

Max gave Grace a curt nod and left the room, his cheeks flushed red with irritation.

"I was hoping you might make a special dish for me tonight," Grace said, clearly aware that the man was making as much noise as he possibly could. "I saw in the brochure that you often will make—"

"That is only with much advance notice!" LeFleur snapped and then turned to the dishwasher. "Get out!"

The young man scurried away, dripping suds and water across the kitchen floor as he fled.

"Yes, well I'm sure you can do this little thing for me," Grace said, pouring on whatever vestiges of charm she felt she still had access to before resorting to threatening to tell management of his unhelpfulness. "I know you have the ingredients and it would mean a lot to me."

LeFleur expelled a noisy burst of air. "What is it?" he said in exasperation.

"A *crème caramel?*" Grace said. "It would mean so much to—"

"I have no fresh fruit."

It took energy on Grace's part to keep her smile in place but she managed to.

It was all she could do to not say "*I know you have fresh fruit! What did you intend to serve at breakfast tomorrow? Rasins?*"

Instead, she continued to smile, "Well, that's fine," she said sweetly. "A drizzle of simple syrup would be lovely."

"Table six," he spat out, tossing down his dishtowel.

"Pardon?"

"Sit at table six so I know where to bring the flan."

"Oh! Thank you," Grace said with relief. *Phase One completed!* "Thank you so much, Chef LeFleur."

She turned and walked out of the dining room, now unmindful of the brooding dark shape of the mountain that filled the display window as she crossed the room. When she reached the lobby she was already mentally sorting out what she would wear to dinner when she heard the shouting.

7

STILL WATERS

Maggie was sipping a small glass of sherry in the lobby when the fireworks started.

She'd showered, dressed for dinner and come down to the lobby to find not a soul there but a very welcoming arrangement of warm *gougères* and bite-sized *tarte flambées*.

It was such a luxury to have her thoughts to herself after nine intense weeks of playing hostess to all the diverse and kinetic personalities in her extended family. She felt a twinge of guilt thinking of Laurent at home still managing them all—only without Maggie's help and with the addition of a bratty teenager.

She took another sip of her sherry and pushed the thought away. It wouldn't help to obsess about what was or wasn't happening back home. And she'd be there soon enough, up to her neck in it herself. This time was for relaxing and by God, Maggie intended to enjoy every precious moment of it.

It was on that thought that the front door swung open, banging loudly on its hinges and a woman charged in, bee-lining to the front desk. The force of her entrance made Maggie look up.

This was no ordinary day-tripper or tourist looking to relax for a few days.

This was a woman with a mission.

She was attractive with short blonde hair, her clothing chic and stylish, and a fabulously expensive pink Hermès scarf knotted at her throat.

So probably French.

The woman banged her fist on the counter bell, destroying all semblance of peace and serenity in the lobby and Maggie instantly felt herself drawing some conclusions about her. Laurent said Maggie tended to make up her mind about people too quickly—and then was reluctant to revise her opinion even in the face of contradictory evidence—so Maggie tried not to dislike the woman on sight.

When the concierge Madame Chaix appeared from the office behind the desk, the French between the two was too rapid for Maggie to follow and she felt dispirited for a moment at the thought that after all these years she still didn't understand the language at the speed of a native.

But what she lacked in vocabulary she was picking up quickly in intention.

The newcomer wanted a room number for someone in the resort and Madame Chaix wasn't having it.

Maggie heard "my husband" and "his whore" and there was much finger pointing in the direction of the upstairs bedrooms.

You don't have to be Miss Marple to figure this one out, Maggie thought.

As the newcomer's voice rose higher and higher more people began to drift into the lobby to see what was going on. Grace appeared too which surprised Maggie. She would have thought Grace would be upstairs napping or fussing with her clothes.

Clothes were very important to Grace.

Finally, it appeared the woman was agreeing to register at the hotel in order to find her wayward husband herself.

Maggie frowned. She didn't want drama these next few days. And this woman clearly was all about drama.

Maggie watched the woman snatch her room key from Madame Chaix and charge up the stairs.

Madame Chaix noted that Maggie was watching and quickly came from behind the counter and approached her. "I am so sorry about that," she said apologetically.

"Should we be expecting a showdown for the night's entertainment?" Maggie asked smiling at her.

"I sincerely hope not," the concierge said. "But I suppose it is possible."

At that moment Grace walked over.

"Mind if I join you for an *apéro*?" Grace asked, sitting and pouring herself a glass of the amber liquid. She looked at Madame Chaix. "So that was interesting."

Maggie sipped her sherry and tried to relax in spite of the fact that her peace had been effectively pulverized.

"It happens from time to time, I'm afraid," Alys said with a sigh.

"Can you tell us who the lucky guy is?" Grace asked. "So we can be someplace else?"

Alys looked over her shoulder as if someone might be listening and then leaned in close, dropping her voice.

"It is Monsieur Toureille," she said.

"Crap," Maggie said. "He's right across the hall from us."

"*Je suis désolé*," Madame Chaix said.

"Do you expect her to make a scene?" Grace asked.

"As you saw," Alys said with resignation. "It is not the favorite part of the job for me and always it is unfortunate for everyone involved."

Maggie guessed Alys Chaix to be in her mid-thirties. She was attractive but when the smile dropped away, she looked tired and unhappy. There was no wedding ring on her finger and Maggie found herself wondering what Madame Chaix's story was.

"Not many kids in the hotel," Maggie ventured.

Alys smiled. "No. They were here over the holidays," she said. "This is a quiet time. Most people have gone back to work."

"Do you have children?" Grace asked, surprising Maggie. It was just like in the old days when they used to read each other's minds. They could interview someone and take turns asking questions because they both just knew where they were going as one.

The concierge's eyes filled with tears and she wiped them quickly away.

"My little boy," she said. "My mother minds him during the ski season."

"That's a long time not to see him," Maggie said. "You must miss him."

"Very much." The woman pulled herself together and smiled at them. "And now I must check with Chef to make sure your first dinner at the resort is a memorable one. You will excuse me?"

Maggie watched her walk away, her high heels sounding like steel pistons moving rhythmically in an engine as she strode across the hardwood floor of the lobby.

"Something on your mind, Maggie?" Grace asked, surprising Maggie again.

Maggie finished her sherry and stood up.

"Nope," she said. "Just going upstairs to see if I can catch Laurent before dinner. See you in there?"

But she didn't wait for Grace's response before turning and making her way upstairs.

Colin Thompson stood in the bar and watched the drama unfold. In his experience, episodes like he'd just witnessed generally amounted to headaches for the hotel management but nothing more than that.

Except of course for those times when they blew up in your face.

He shifted his stance where he stood leaning into the bar, a scotch and soda in his hand. Once the shrieking Frenchie had stomped upstairs he'd been mere moments away from approaching the American woman. She was younger than him by at least ten years, maybe more, and she wore a wedding band, but in Colin's experience, that didn't always mean anything.

She was a sexy thing, he thought as he watched her now as she spoke with Madame Chaix. Not a demure bone in her body that he could see. Very take charge. Typical American but he liked that in a woman. He liked to see them walk into a situation and move to the head of the queue so to speak. This woman was no exception. And one thing Colin knew—if not through experience than because it just stood to reason—a take charge woman out of bed was a take charge woman in bed too.

What better time to experience something like that—a fantasy for him on every level—than with both of them on their own at a romantic French ski chalet and no one the wiser when the week was done?

While he hadn't exactly envisioned someone like Madame Derne-yur—or *Maggie* as he'd overheard her friend call her—in his wildest dreams, that didn't mean it couldn't happen. He felt his heart race at the thought and for the first time since he'd been unceremoniously escorted from the building at his last job he found himself wishing he had someone back home that he'd be able to tell the tale to.

He threw back the rest of his drink—his third—and licked his lips. The concierge was still talking with Maggie which would make his asking to the join them all the easier. And then the concierge would leave—after all she was working—and Bob was your bleeding uncle. He smoothed down the wool jumper over his protruding belly which reminded him to suck it in a bit and was seconds from walking across the lobby to where the women were when the other American woman appeared as if out of nowhere.

Colin stopped abruptly and edged his way back to the bar, his eyes on the woman as she floated across the lobby and then stood talking to Maggie. It occurred to him that she might not sit down and he could still have his moment but that hope died quickly as the goddess took her seat by his prey and poured herself a sherry.

Just staring at the blonde made Colin's heart race. She looked like she'd stepped out of a movie. And every man's fantasy.

How is it possible for one person to be that perfect?

She was talking intently to Maggie now and crossing her legs. Colin's eye followed the movement of those legs, and watched the drape of her skirt as she plucked at it to arrange it higher across her knees and he felt himself becoming aroused. Blushing furiously at the effect the woman was having on him, he turned to the man behind the bar and ordered another scotch whiskey.

Now was not a good time for this. He knew the two American women weren't sharing a room so he'd have another opportunity. He turned to watch them and saw Maggie stand up.

Holding his whiskey to his lips, his eyes followed her as she turned and left the lobby, taking the stairs to her bedroom, her hips moving quickly under her slim skirt. When he glanced back at the other woman—Grace her name was—he saw she was holding her glass of sherry and staring out the window. He was surprised to realize she looked sad.

Am I not giving myself full credit? he thought with sudden wonderment.

Is it possible I might stand a chance with her?

He downed the rest of his drink and watched her, knowing he wouldn't have the nerve to approach her. At least not yet. For now, watching her was enough.

Could he imagine her saying yes to him? To kissing him? Inviting him into her hotel room?

He rubbed an agitated hand across his face and forced

himself not to order another drink. His legs were jelly as it was. If he had any hope of a chance with that amazing creature he'd need to be in full possession of his faculties. He licked his lips again at the notion.

After all, just because Rosie was a lying cheating whore of a wife, didn't mean all women were.

8

BLACK AND BLUE DAYS

The late afternoon breeze whipped dead leaves into a whirling vortex of dust and twigs along the tractor road that dissected Laurent's vineyards. It was probably too cold to have Jemmy working to prune the vines but it might do him good just the same. Laurent shifted his phone to his other ear and squinted into the distance toward the edge of his land, marked by the country road that led to the village.

"Laurent?" Maggie said on the other line. "Are you listening to me?"

"Of course, *chérie*," he said. "I was just thinking."

"I mean, Grace is doing everything short of offering to give me a daily manicure and a massage."

"She wants to make amends."

"Like I would ever forgive her for what she did."

"That is not like you, *chérie*. Perhaps you should give her a chance."

"I can't believe *you're* telling me that," Maggie said. "You were furious with Grace after she lied to us about the photographer and then she let Mila get nabbed."

"Yes, of course, like any parent, I was upset," Laurent said mildly. "But Grace is your friend."

"*Was* my friend."

Laurent had been pleased when Maggie called. But he felt a twinge of disquiet at how resistant she seemed to be to making peace with Grace. He knew his wife. He knew she wouldn't be happy if she didn't forgive Grace. Whether or not she opted to go forward with the friendship was another thing. But she needed to let go of her frustration with her.

Laurent glanced down one of the long lines of the vineyard. Jemmy had a habit of disappearing and it was easy enough to do in the big field.

"As you say, *chérie*," he said. "But it is not for Grace that I suggest it."

"For me? You think I need her?"

"Of course not. End the friendship if you want. That is up to you. I only know that you will not be happy if you turn her away *as you are doing*."

"I disagree. I think it's the only way I can do it. Like ripping a Band-Aid off. I don't even know why I agreed to come on this trip. Except for the skiing."

"*D'accord*. Then there is nothing more to say. Will you ski tomorrow?"

"If the weather cooperates. The ski instructor thinks there might be too much snow coming."

"Ah, you are having the handsome ski instructor?"

"Well, I'm not exactly *having* him and I think he was a lot more handsome back around the time when Twiggy used to ski here."

Laurent laughed and then caught sight of Jemmy breaking the vines instead of marking the withered ones for pruning as he'd been instructed. Laurent felt a rush of annoyance spread through him.

"Love you, Laurent. I'll call the kids later tonight," Maggie said. "Dinner time here. Gotta run."

"*Bon. Je t'aime aussi, chérie*," Laurent said as he disconnected. "Jem!" he called to his son.

Jemmy looked up, a scarlet blush of guilt spreading across his face.

What is the matter with the boy? Is he attempting to deliberately provoke me?

A burst of swear words erupted into the air and Laurent turned to see Zouzou sitting on the ground by the fence examining her nails.

This is the reason, he thought—briefly undecided as to which child to address first. It had taken Zouzou nearly an hour to plod her way home the mile distance from where Laurent had let her out of the car yesterday. She'd stomped into the house and gone straight to her room—relieving Laurent of the task of sending her there. While he'd sent Jem up to make her aware that dinner was being served an hour later, she refused to come out.

Their housekeeper, Marie-Claire, had already mentioned the candy wrappers she'd found in Zouzou's bedroom closet.

He strode over to where Zouzou sat on the ground.

"Get up," he said when he reached her.

She glared up at him. "I scratched my finger," she said.

He reached down and took her by the front of her jacket and hauled her to her feet.

"Hey! You can't touch me! It's against the law."

Laurent's nostrils flared but he released her. "I can of course put you down the well on my own property and leave you there for the rest of the day," he said calmly. "In France that is not against the law."

He felt a flicker of guilt when he saw her eyes widen as the momentary fear passed through her.

"Mom would kill you," she said. "You can't do that."

"Go back to the house. Your foul words pollute the air and frighten the birds."

"But I'm tired of being stuck in my room."

Laurent turned as if to lay hands on her again and she jumped away and jogged toward the house.

"I'm going," she said over her shoulder. "But I'm telling my Mom what you did."

That is good, Laurent thought as he watched her trudge back to the house. *At least she believes her mother still cares.*

Then, as he turned to deal with Jemmy, Laurent saw two figures approaching them through the far side of the vineyard. From where he stood he could see Jean-Luc's car parked on the village road which separated Laurent's vineyard from Jean-Luc's.

Laurent raised a hand to greet them as the couple made their way painstakingly through the vineyard toward them.

"*Bonjour,* Laurent," Jean-Luc called. As yesterday, Jean-Luc looked frail but Laurent was glad to see him out and about.

"*Pépère!*" Jemmy cried and ran to Jean-Luc. He reached him and threw himself into Jean-Luc's arms, nearly knocking the old man to the ground. Danielle braced Jean-Luc and the two of them wrapped their arms around Jemmy in greeting.

Jean-Luc was wearing faded canvas overalls and heavy leather shoes. He used a cane that Laurent had never seen before and the sight of it sent a spasm of dismay through Laurent.

"Getting a little exercise?" Laurent asked as he greeted the pair and kissed Danielle on both cheeks.

"We decided it's been too long since Jean-Luc has seen the children," Danielle said.

"Where have you been, *Pépère?*" Jemmy asked.

"Oh, here and there, *mon chou,*" Jean-Luc asked, his eyes glittering with amusement and fondness as he regarded the boy.

"We have had a break-in," Danielle said.

Laurent frowned. "When?"

"It is nothing," Jean-Luc said. "Women always dramatize

everything. Some tools were taken from my potting shed," Jean-Luc said.

"Very valuable?" Laurent asked.

"No, not at all. But still."

It was unusual to have thefts in the area. They weren't close to a major town and the area was populated by hard-working farmers for the most part. Laurent tried to think if he'd ever heard of many of thefts since he'd come to St-Buvard almost ten years earlier.

"Just keep your eyes open," Jean-Luc said. "And your doors locked."

"Oh, here comes your in-laws," Danielle said. "I can't believe I haven't seen John since he arrived."

Laurent turned to see Elspeth walking through the back terrace of the house with Mila. Behind them, John Newberry walked solemnly, his head down.

It had been nearly a year since he and Maggie and the children had been back to Atlanta to see the Newberrys. Even then, Laurent had noticed the worrisome differences in John.

"Hello, Jean-Luc! Danielle!" Elspeth called out as she set Mila down. The little girl ran to the elderly French couple as they released Jemmy.

"*Bonjour* Elspeth!" Jean-Luc called back.

Laurent joined the two couples as they shook hands with Elspeth. John hung back, his gaze directed downward, his face flushed.

"*Bonjour*, John," Jean-Luc said but John didn't respond.

"He's just tired," Elspeth said lightly. "He just woke up from his morning nap, didn't you, darling? How are you feeling, Jean-Luc?"

"I'm very good, *merci*," Jean-Luc said.

"I'm not tired!" John said petulantly. "You said we were coming out for ice cream. Jemmy and I are to have ice cream for our lunch."

Jean-Luc exchanged a glance with Laurent.

"Yes, darling," Elspeth said, "but Jemmy is helping his father in the vineyard right now. Aren't you, Jemmy?"

Before the child could respond, John cursed loudly—using a word the children had rarely heard in their house. "Damn this vineyard!" John said. "You told me he was selling the damn thing!"

This time Danielle looked at Laurent and all he could do was give a barely perceptible shake of his head.

"All in due time, darling," Elspeth said, the strain showing on her face as she took a hold of John's arm and began to tug him back toward the house. "Why don't we see what kind of ice cream there is in the—"

"Jemmy must come too," John said.

"But I want to stay with *Pépère*," Jemmy said, reaching for Jean-Luc's hand. "We're working in the vineyard, aren't we, *Pépère*?"

"Well, yes, we—" Jean-Luc started to say as he looked from Elspeth's face to Laurent's, unsure of how to handle the coming crisis.

"No!" John roared. "I am Jemmy's grandfather, not you! He will come with me to have ice cream!" John's eyes were glittering with fury as he took a step toward Jean-Luc. Even though he was frail and leaning on a cane, Jean-Luc never moved. Laurent took his father-in-law by the arm and gently held him in place.

"I think we might all go inside to have ice cream," Laurent said evenly, his eyes on Elspeth.

"No! Jemmy is my grandson! This bastard has stolen him from me!"

"Elspeth?" Laurent said firmly. "Do you want me to take him back?"

John jerked his arm away from Laurent and turned on his heel. "That bastard better know that Jemmy belongs to me, not him!" he shouted over his shoulder.

Laurent let out a breath of air as John stumbled his way back through the vineyard toward the *mas*. Elspeth surprised Laurent by turning to him before following John. She grabbed his arm, her nails digging into his skin.

"I am too old to do this by myself," she hissed. "I cannot raise Nicole and deal with him too. Maggie must come home!"

She shot an arm out to point to the surrounding vineyard, its desiccated wintry presentation of grape vines, like a military graveyard of crosses.

"This...this is a fantasy," she said. "But that man is Maggie's father and *he* is real. He needs her. *I* need her."

She released his arm and turned to hurry after John.

"Laurent, I am so sorry," Danielle said. "I had no idea."

Laurent waved away her words. "None of us did really."

Jean-Luc had taken both children and walked away to focus on a particularly robust rootstock.

"Will you really leave St-Buvard?" she asked.

Laurent felt a hollowness in his chest.

Was Elspeth right? Did Maggie not have a right to her own life if her parents needed her?

"I don't know," he said.

Danielle patted Laurent on the arm and turned to join Jean-Luc and the children. At one point, Jean-Luc straightened up and looked at the house where John and Elspeth had just entered. He put a hand on Jemmy's head and spoke to the child and Laurent heard Jemmy's voice, high and insistent.

"No, it's not fair. I never see you any more!"

Jean-Luc patted Jemmy's head and then knelt to say a few words to Mila. As Laurent watched he saw Jean-Luc point something out to Jemmy and the boy instantly responded. Laurent shook his head in amazement.

Jemmy had resisted everything Laurent had asked him to do in the vineyard all morning long but the boy was so connected to Jean-Luc that it only took a few words and the child was interested in pruning or doing whatever Jean-Luc suggested without hesitation.

As the pair moved deeper into the vineyard with the children, Laurent could hear his son laughing and he realized it had been a while since he'd heard Jemmy laugh. Jemmy was a strong-willed child. Kind and sweet but with a mind of his own. The boy's tendency to resist him made Laurent proud at the same time it discouraged him. *Seven was awfully young for a son to be already fighting his papa.*

As Laurent's eyes skimmed the contour of his land he wondered how it was that after a lifetime of working the land, living the land, Jean-Luc could turn away from it and leave. How was that possible?

And as he thought that he realized that he himself no longer knew what the land meant to him any more. Through all the years of trials and experimenting, struggle and hope, he never stopped to think or wonder if this was still what he wanted.

And now, he found himself wondering if the most loving thing he could do for Maggie was to leave all this.

9

BEFORE THE DELUGE

That evening Maggie was the first one downstairs. She knew she probably should have knocked on Grace's door but she didn't so that was that. She also knew that Grace was probably starting to see her as very unfriendly but she couldn't help how she felt, could she?

Clearly Laurent thought she could and it was annoying that he felt she should hold out the hand of friendship to Grace after everything that had happened. He was as angry at Grace as Maggie had been but now he thought she should forgive her?

Maggie felt a spasm of guilt for not asking Laurent more about how he was getting along with her parents. He hadn't mentioned Zouzou at all on top of which Maggie knew Jemmy was trying to press his father's buttons.

And then there was her mother.

Why her mom felt she needed to hit Maggie with this now of all times! But of course, Maggie knew it wasn't a matter of Elspeth choosing her time. Maggie's father was sick. Her mother needed her. It was that simple.

Maggie wore a basic crewneck cashmere sweater set in grey over wool slacks She felt much more relaxed than she had earlier.

She had to admit that a hot shower, the afternoon sherry, and touching base with Laurent had all come together to help her feel that way—relaxed and ready for a pleasant evening.

Half way down the stairs, she saw Max Fountainbleu dressed as a waiter.

"*Bonsoir*, Monsieur Fontainbleau," she said.

He nodded but she could tell he was in a hurry. They walked to the dining room together.

"Any news on the weather?" Maggie asked.

"*Non*, Madame," Fountainbleu said. "But is bad I think."

Maggie sighed. From the moment she'd sat in the lobby with her sherry looking out of the big bay window she could tell that the weather was worsening. The blowing snow had already plastered thick crusts of hoarfrost on the windows that faced the front drive.

As she entered the dining room she noticed the painted crown molding on the ceiling was peeling giving off a sense of restrained shabbiness. A giant crystal chandelier swung gently over the entrance.

She remembered that Grace had said that they were to sit at table six.

"Table six?" she said to Max. He quickly led her to a round table set for four closest to the lobby entrance.

Maggie seated herself but she was annoyed. There were at least two tables by the picture window facing the mountain. And while it was true you couldn't see anything at this time of night, if they were to keep the same table—as was the custom—throughout their stay then they were going to have a very poor view from this table.

The sweaty-faced Englishman that they'd met earlier approached her tentatively, his dinner plate and his napkin in his hand..

"Good evening," he said. "I was wondering...it's just that I'm alone tonight."

Maggie gestured to the chair next to hers. "Be my guest," she said.

He settled into the chair clutching his napkin and then seemed to realize he now had two.

"I'm Colin Thompson of Brighton," he said.

"Maggie Dernier."

Maggie wondered briefly what Mr. Thompson's story was. He was too old and out of shape to be a skier. Plus, he was alone.

"Hello, darling," Grace said as she swept into the room.

Thompson immediately jumped to his feet, knocking over his chair in the process.

"Hello, you," Grace said to him. "Joining us?"

"If...if that's all right," he stuttered.

"Perfectly all right," Grace said breezily.

Maggie tried to discern if Grace really thought it was all right. After all, she knew that Grace wanted to have several very serious talks with her. It was likely she'd been looking forward to kicking off those talks tonight.

If so, too bad.

"Mr. Thompson is from Brighton," Maggie said, looking around the dining room. The Indian couple was at their same table by the window and closest to the swinging doors of the kitchen.

The table directly in front of the plate glass window through which Maggie could only assume would provide an amazing view of the mountain in the morning held the faux Madame Toureille, sitting alone, reading a hardback book.

Seeing her sitting there by herself reminded Maggie that there were likely to be emotional fireworks later. She wondered if the real Madame Toureille had found Monsieur Toureille.

She scrutinized the face of the woman sitting alone at the table to try to discern if she looked upset. Her face was unperturbed and calm as she turned the pages of her book. She didn't look up as one might who was expecting to be joined by a companion.

Very strange.

Max Fountainbleu came to the Indian couple's table and poured water for them before moving to the table of Monsieur Toureile's girlfriend.

"So Mr. Thompson," Grace said breezily, "what brings you to *Chalet Savoir Faire* all by your lonesome?"

"I quite like your American turn of phrase," Thompson said, breathing heavily as he dabbed at the water sweating on his glass. "I suppose I stick out like a sore digit."

"I take it you're not here training for the World Cup?" Grace said.

Maggie had to hand it to Grace. She had the knack for inane gab. Laurent was always fussing at Maggie for not chatting more with their neighbors or the people in the village of St-Buvard. Maggie couldn't help that she always wanted to get to the point. But she'd long ago learned the hard way how important idle chatter leading up to the meat of things was in a rural or small town setting.

"Oh, no," Thompson said, grinning and blinking until he was pink in the face. "I'd have to say my talents lie elsewhere."

"Do tell."

"I'm a retired policeman, you see."

"Indeed?" Grace smiled coolly at him over her water glass. When Max came to take their orders, she didn't even look up, just continued to smile at Thompson. "I'll just have whatever the house specialty is, darling," she said.

"Me too," Maggie said closing her menu. Laurent would want to know what she ate and he wouldn't be amused to hear it was grilled cheese or whatever *poulet* the resort had on offer. As a chef in his own right, Laurent was constantly urging her to take culinary chances or, failing that, to at least go with the chef's specialty. He seemed to think even a mystery dish prepared by a proper French cook was better than anything Maggie might cherry-pick off the menu.

"So," Grace said to Thompson after Max left. "You're a little young for retirement, surely?"

Thompson blushed and looked down at his hands as he fiddled with his fork. Maggie thought he looked uncomfortable if pleased by Grace's comment that he looked young. Even so, most cops Maggie knew were not the nervous type. They did not twiddle or fidget with their serving ware. If anything they were preternaturally self-assured.

"There was an issue," he said softly. "Not a biggie by any means. But they edged me out over it."

Maggie glanced again at the table of Monsieur Toureille's girlfriend and decided she must not be expecting him, since she'd already ordered her meal.

The Indian couple was speaking to each other in loud voices now. Or at least the guy was. The woman, who was dressed not in traditional Indian garb but in a bland cardigan sweater buttoned to her chin, sat with her head down, her hands in her lap while her husband animatedly addressed her.

"What a jerk," Maggie said as she watched him.

Thompson turned in his seat and snorted in disgust. "*Wogs,*" he said.

Maggie was surprised at the racial slur but before she could say anything her attention was caught by the motion of the young Indian husband jumping up and storming into the kitchen.

His wife clapped a horrified hand to her mouth and looked around the dining room as if to gauge how much attention they were calling to themselves.

"He sure does seem to have a problem with the food here," Maggie said, watching the swinging kitchen doors and then turning to Grace. "Wasn't he upset about something with the chef at lunch too when we came in earlier?"

"I've dealt with packi's before," Thompson said disdainfully. "They're impossible on every level. Trust me."

Sorry now that she'd invited Thompson to their table even if it meant she and Grace were saved from an intimate conversation, Maggie turned back to her place setting wondering how long before she could eat and claim a headache and leave. She glanced at her watch. If she got back to the room by eight the kids would still be up and she could say goodnight.

"Maggie?" Grace asked.

"I'm sorry, what?" Maggie looked around.

"Detective Thompson was asking how long you were married."

"Going on nine years," Maggie said. "And you?"

"Nearly twenty," he said. "Which is why it came as such a shock when the ball and chain chucked me out."

"Oh, dear. I can't imagine why," Grace murmured and Maggie nearly smiled.

Grace had the right view on how to handle this guy, Maggie decided. Not too seriously, that's for sure. Just when Maggie determined she'd be able to enjoy the rest of her evening in spite of the Englishman, she saw the Indian man return to his table and reseat himself. Within seconds, his wife burst into tears and fled the room.

Without thinking Maggie stood up and then quickly sat back down again, hearing Laurent's voice admonishing her as clearly as if he were in the room with her—to stay out of it. She didn't know what the young man had said to the poor woman but she could guess.

Why do some men act like that? she thought, grinding her teeth in barely suppressed fury.

"Oy!" the Indian man yelled after his wife. "Don't be like that, ye stupid cow! You're causing a scene!"

Maggie and Grace exchanged a glance and Maggie realized it was nice to communicate with someone where you didn't have to use words to get your meaning across. She and Laurent did that to a certain extent but not nearly so well as she used to be able to do it with Grace.

Maggie felt a quick, undefinable twinge of loss before shaking off the sensation and turning her attention with breezy nonchalance to the now-perspiring middle-aged English detective seated at their table.

10

INTO THE STORM

Max watched the scene through the small round window in the swinging doors that separated the kitchen and the dining room. He was glad to see the young Indian woman leave the table but sorry to see her in tears as she did.

He narrowed his eyes as he watched her husband shouting after her. It took all his will not to go into the dining room and knock the *bâtard* on his *derriere*.

He took in a sharp intake of breath to calm himself. He'd already had too many witnesses to his bad temper today. One more example of it—this time for the whole dining room to witness—would not be prudent.

"What are you doing, you hopeless *idiot*?" a voice snarled in Max's ear, making him jump.

When would he learn not to turn his back on LeFleur? Even if LeFleur wasn't intending to insert a knife in his back, it never served him well to forget about the bastard.

"I have filled all the water glasses," Max said mildly, not bothering to turn around. He could feel the man behind him shifting away. The clattering sound of a pan being placed aggressively on the stove confirmed that LeFleur had indeed moved away.

Max turned to glance behind him. The kitchen was empty except for the two of them. There weren't enough guests to keep on a full staff at this point in the season and most of the dishes that LeFleur was preparing were frozen anyway.

Top notch Parisian chef indeed, Max thought sourly as he watched LeFleur empty a packet of dried gravy mix into a pan of water. *What a farce. I cook better than this connard.*

LeFleur scratched his head and looked around his kitchen before snatching up a wooden spoon.

"Get over here and stir this," LeFleur barked at Max. "Make yourself useful."

In the old days, Max would never have interacted with the kitchen help—the chef included. In the old days, he would be seated out there in the dining room discussing the day of skiing over wine and fondue with any of a number of the young female guests.

In the old days.

"Fountainbleu? Have you gone deaf in your old age? Get over here!"

Max moved away from his vantage point at the door and edged toward the stove where LeFleur stood brandishing the spoon.

What does Alys see in this ape? How can she possibly care for him?

Just the thought of Alys in this man's arms—sweaty and doughy from lack of any real physical labor or exercise—made Max's stomach lurch as if he would lose his lunch right here on the kitchen floor.

"You think you're too good for this, don't you?" LeFleur said, shoving the spoon into Max's hand before turning to go to the freezer where Max knew he would get the mass-manufactured *poulet Kievs* that he bought for the resort in individual portions.

LeFleur was right about one thing though, Max thought, with a heavy heart as he stared down at his hands.

He would never have been subjected to this treatment even ten years ago. Twenty years ago? The women fell at his feet and slipped their hotel room keys to him— sometimes right in front of their husbands! In those days he could have had *five* Alys's—all at the same time in his room if he wanted!

He stabbed the spoon into the powdery substance in the pot and tried to break up the lumps.

Should he have married? Had a few kids? It had seemed insensible back then. *Give up this sexual playground to be henpecked by one woman? Inconceivable.* Somehow he just never saw the day when he would be helping in the kitchen, handing out menus and carrying luggage upstairs.

Worse than that, the kind of women who used to throw themselves at him back then—now they didn't even see him. He was the wallpaper, a functionary role. A robot to get their bags upstairs, an automaton to take their meal orders.

He didn't exist for them now.

He felt a heaviness in his limbs and a sudden urgent desire to be alone came over him.

"If that gravy burns I'll have you shoveling the front drive in a snow storm," LeFleur sneered as he walked past Max with a tray full of the Cellophane topped meals in plastic cartons.

Max stirred the gravy, watching the granular lumps of the mix as they dissolved in the water and he didn't know who he hated more—LeFleur for his bullying and his smugness over being with the beautiful Alys, or himself for everything he'd lost that he'd never seen coming.

He turned to watch LeFleur as he tossed the frozen packages into the microwave oven. The creature paused to slip his hand into the back of his trousers to scratch his bare ass before reaching for one of the baguettes that lay on the counter.

"Slice this up when you're done with that," LeFleur said, not looking at Max. "And get them in baskets and on the tables. You should have done it before now."

Before Max could answer, LeFleur swung around, his head twisting to look around the kitchen.

"The *bourguignon* is still not served?" he said with incredulity, his mouth open.

Max could see the silver-domed tray on the counter by the door. His stomach roiled at the realization.

Merde. He'd been so distracted by the Indian couple fighting that he'd forgotten to bring Table Five their food!

LeFleur turned to look at him and what Max saw on his face was not outrage or even surprise but triumph. This was the death knell for Max. He knew it and LeFleur knew it.

LeFleur had already been complaining to management that Max was too old to handle any of his tasks around the chalet.

Complaining to Alys after lovemaking?

Max hurried over to the meal tray, refusing to meet LeFleur's eyes.

"You know what this means, don't you?" LeFleur said as Max picked up the tray and hurried to the swinging door.

Yes, Max knew. He knew he would now have to do something he'd hoped he wouldn't have to. Something desperate to stop the downward spiral of his life. Something to stop the taunts and jeers from LeFleur.

Something he'd never thought himself capable of before.

Alys sat in her office behind the registration desk. She knew she should be in the dining room greeting guests, making sure the staff saw her, making sure they were giving their best to the paying customers.

The staff. There was only Max and Denis tonight. One had

her, one wanted her. They both hated each other. How had she let it get to this?

Alys shifted painfully in her chair and pulled at the waist-band of her ski pants to look at the bruise on her hip. Denis had been too rough again last night. However many times she warned him...no, not a warning. She'd asked him. He'd ignored her.

If she wanted to be with him, this was just the way it was.

Do I? she asked herself. She was breathing shallowly and felt a persistent creep of fatigue up her arms. *Do I want to be with him? Why?*

She stood up and turned off her desk lamp and scanned the empty lobby. There were now only five couples currently staying in the chalet—and two of those gone out to dinner tonight in the village.

She pulled her polyester cardigan tighter around her. Denis didn't like her clothes. Didn't like the slick coarseness of the poly-ester suits that she wore. He felt she looked too severe in them. But polyester was all she could afford.

Was she with Denis because he was so much like Etienne? The thought wasn't a new one. Both were so confident and masculine, so in control of every situation—and of her too.

And look how things had turned out with Etienne, she thought bitterly. A painful divorce, a restraining order and an endless roster of lies to their child.

Well, she couldn't be sorry she'd known Etienne. How could she? She had Jean-Marc as a result of knowing him. A twinge of fear evaded her gut. Why wasn't Jean-Marc getting better? The doctor said *possibly* epilepsy but the doctor also said they should be seeing improvement by now.

She put the worries out of her mind as forcefully as she could and scanned her desk before leaving her office. She wasn't sure why she was hesitating except for the fact that as soon as she stepped into that dining room, she would need to play the part of the cheerful, accommodating hostess. The smile would be in place as she greeted the guests. The warmth in her voice couldn't sound forced or in any way artificial as she assured them that she would do everything in her power to make them happy and comfortable.

And who will do that for me? a small voice whispered in her head.

Already she'd noticed that the act had become harder and harder to pull off. Lately, every time a woman walked through the front door wearing fur or cashmere, her Louis Vuitton train case dangling casually from one hand while poor Max struggled with the rest, Alys wanted to pull out a machine gun and saturate the lobby with her haughty and very red blood.

She saw that her hands were shaking slightly and she stood for a moment in the lobby.

Everyone would be so shocked to know I had such a thought. Even Denis would be shocked although probably not appalled. He hated the guests even more than she did.

Sounds came to her from the dining room and she turned in that direction, not able to delay her entrance a moment longer and realizing that imagining the bloody destruction of every smug entitled, and self-righteous rich bitch sitting in that room was probably not the best attitude to have right now if she wanted to pull off the charade for one more night.

11

THE DEVIL'S DEAL

By the time Laurent got all the children in the car and headed toward the village a fine haze was beginning to bleach the sky a pale blue. Dinner had been a shambles the night before and while Laurent had again resorted to banishing Zouzou to her room so that the rest of them could eat in peace, he still had to go up and tell her to turn down her music.

On his second trip upstairs, he took all objects in the room that might in any way produce music or noise of any kind and handed her a sandwich which she snatched from him, screaming "I hate you!" before he left the room.

As children will, both Mia and Jemmy had picked up on the tension in the house and began to act up themselves. The mood likewise affected whatever was happening with Laurent's father-in-law. Still pouting over the incident in the vineyard the day before, John alternately glowered at everyone or fawned over his grandson to the obvious exclusion of little Mila who ended up in tears by the end of the meal and fussy in her grandmother's lap.

Was it possible that Zouzou's bad attitude was affecting everyone? Before the night was over, Jemmy had been sent to bed in tears for refusing to pick up his toys in the salon, and John Newberry had shouted at Elspeth that she was smothering him. *Which, to be fair...*

And then of course there was the tension between Laurent and Elspeth. While she'd apologized for what she'd said to him in the vineyard and how she'd said it, Laurent knew that her feelings hadn't changed. She wanted Maggie to come back to Atlanta to help her with John's declining mental health and clearly she believed that if Laurent loved Maggie he would support this move.

At Elpseth's suggestion after breakfast—a meal punctuated by more tears and protests—Laurent agreed that an outing would help everyone take a breath and settle down. Just getting out of the house tended to have that effect on him and he didn't see why it wouldn't help three cranky children. He had to draw the line over bringing John, however. There was every chance of running into Jean-Luc at Le Canard, the village bar and café, and Laurent didn't want to court any more trouble than he could already count on.

The village of St-Buvard was perched on the side of a hill with the remains of a Roman aqueduct at its base. There was one *charcuterie*, one tiny post office, and one café. The *boulangerie* that had been shuttered years ago had since been briefly opened by a family of Americans and turned into a bistro. The brutal murder of its owner and chef had closed it within a week of opening. In the interim two years there had been some effort to recreate it as another *boulangerie*—something the village badly needed—but no attempt had succeeded for longer than a few weeks.

After parking his car, Laurent instructed Jemmy and Zouzou to stay together and meet him at Le Canard in thirty minutes. The village didn't have much in the way of shop windows to peruse but it would give both children a sense of freedom and independence that he could not afford to give them in reality. He settled Mila down at one of the indoor tables in the café Le Canard.

Inside the café there were only five tables and nobody— unless it was sleeting or very cold as it presently was—ever sat there. In the summer, its outdoor terrace would be full. The terrace spilled out directly onto the village square through which ran the winding main street that dissected the village.

In the fall, the entire square was littered with leaves from the large plantain trees that lined the terrace. The cobblestones were rough and uneven—probably the original stones from hundreds of years earlier.

Today, he and Mila joined only three other people in the café. As Laurent settled Mila in her chair with her iPad and a game, he smiled sadly. Le Canard had always delighted his father-in-law who always mentioned it with eager anticipation every time he visited them. John had been in France four weeks now without mentioning it once.

Gaspard Theroux, the proprietor of Le Canard, came to Laurent's table and thumped down a glass of *pastis*. While Laurent wouldn't call Theroux a friend exactly, he'd spent enough hours at his café in the last nine years to know him well.

"*Bonjour*, Laurent," Theroux said. "And what will the little one have? Hot chocolate?"

"*Oui, s'il vous plaît*," Mila said.

Theroux withdrew and Laurent nodded at the three other men in the café. Through the dusty café window he could see both Zouzou and Jemmy wandering down the main street looking in the shop windows. Zouzou's father Windsor had alluded to some minor problems with Zouzou but his hands were —as usual—full of Taylor's much bigger problems and he'd not given Laurent the full picture of Zouzou's issues.

"*Alors*, Laurent," a man nearby, a retired farmer named Remy said. "I hear Jean-Luc is moving to the Côte d'Azur. Can this be true?"

Laurent smiled amiably. It was his policy to neither confirm nor deny any gossip or information he did not know for a fact was public knowledge.

"I have heard the same rumor," Laurent said noncommittally, sipping his *pastis*.

Theroux set a mug of cocoa down in front of Mila. Flakes of shaved chocolate were sprinkled over the dollop of fresh cream that bobbed on top.

"*Merci, Monsieur*," Mila said, reaching for the drink.

"I heard that Domaine St-Buvard was for sale, too," Remy said. The other men at the table turned expectedly to Laurent. While Laurent may understandably dissemble on gossip about someone else, it would be marginally more difficult to do it about his own situation.

"Where did you hear that?" Laurent asked.

They all shrugged.

It was true that Laurent had made a few discreet inquiries about the viability of selling Domaine St-Buvard. He should have known it would get back to the village. While these old fellows probably didn't surf the Internet for their news, they had other more dependable sources of information.

"So is it true?" Theroux asked from where he stood by Laurent's table.

"No," Laurent said. But something in the way he answered sounded even to his own ears as if he'd left space for the words *not yet*.

"Have you heard about the American bistro?" Theroux asked, gesturing toward the shuttered restaurant down the street. "It is for sale again."

Laurent had noticed the *For Sale* sign in the window. He hoped the owners were doing something more than just letting the villagers know their intent to sell since no more than a hundred people were likely to see the sign in the window. But something tingled his senses as he glanced down the street in the direction of the bistro.

It had been Madame Renoir's bakery once years ago. Even then it had been little more than a fallen down wreck of a place. Since then it had been renovated beyond what a simple country village could support. The bistro it had become was made to look intentionally rustic, meaning the owners had spent a fortune to affect a look of age that the interior already in fact had.

Inside the bistro was a gleaming maple-top bar that stretched the entire width of the restaurant with open shelving separating the kitchen—the epitome of gastronomical accomplishment which at one point had featured all the latest culinary equipment —from the rustic country dining room.

The picture window in front bore the words *Le Petit Chat Bistro* written across it in elaborate cursive. Laurent heard the owners had paid a ridiculous three thousand euros for it.

"There were never enough people to support such a thing," Theroux said when Laurent didn't respond. "Americans."

Laurent could see Theroux stiffen as he remembered too late that of course Laurent was married to an American.

"I didn't mean—" Theroux said but Laurent waved away his apology.

"*Pas important*," he said but Theroux's words reminded Laurent that he had yet to get in touch with Maggie. He'd tried to call her this morning but his call had gone straight to voice mail. He patted his pockets in search of his cellphone but realized he must have left it back at the house.

He wondered if Elspeth had spoken to Maggie about her wish that Maggie come back to the States with her. If she had, Maggie hadn't said anything about it to Laurent.

Laurent's thoughts drifted back to the vineyard. Regardless of how well he had done with it, he knew it still didn't make enough to break even. If it weren't for Aunt Delphine's money and

Maggie's Provençal newsletter where she advertised local artisans and farmers' goods, he wouldn't be supporting his family.

He stared at the cloudy amber liquid in his glass and swirled it gently. Things felt like he was at a crossroads. One that John Newberry's obvious dementia seemed to be forcing a direction for all of them to go.

Laurent's eye was caught by the movement of two little girls walking together down the street and he realized that one of the girls was Zouzou. He didn't recognize the other child. She was older, dirtier, as if perhaps her people were gypsies. While he watched them in earnest conversation, the door to the café opened and Jemmy came in and sat at their table.

"Hey," he said when he saw Mila's cocoa. "I want one."

Laurent nodded at the door. "Go tell Zouzou to meet us at the car in five minutes," he said as he drained his drink. Jemmy begrudgingly got up and let himself back out.

Perhaps it was time to sell and move on.

Jemmy wouldn't care. Would Maggie?

Maybe Elspeth was right. Family should come first. Laurent hadn't learned that himself growing up but he still knew it to be true. Now more than ever.

And sometimes making family come first required sacrifice.

12

THE PERFECT STORM

R aj sat alone at his dining table and felt the stares like white hot lasers burning into the back of his head from the other diners. Some didn't even bother lowering their voices as they snickered and commented on the dog's dinner his bride had just made at their table.

He would kill her for this. He would kill her for humiliating him like this. And not just her but Dev, his older brother, who'd joked before the wedding that Raj had still ended up with Dev's hand-me-downs—a remark that could only be interpreted one way!

Raj didn't know if it was possible—how it could be possible? —that Dev had slept with Aishwarya before the wedding but he knew that when he'd confronted her with it just now she was not at all convincing in her denials.

I'll kill that bastard when I get back. And I'll deal with my bride long before then.

It had been a continuing source of irritation to Raj that unlike himself Dev got to choose his bride—a beautiful and sexy Indian model who adored Dev and waited on him hand and foot—while Raj was forced into an arranged marriage. Raj hadn't even laid eyes on the cow except for the one time before they'd gotten married! If it weren't for the fact that she had a halfway decent body he would have backed out of it.

A niggling reminder in the back of his mind argued that he wouldn't at all have backed out of anything. His father was a business associate of Aishwarya's family and there had been a tidy settlement on Raj for agreeing to the union.

But that didn't mean he hadn't been well and truly done to!

He'd not been allowed to even meet Aishwarya until it was practically too late. And he could understand why. If he'd met her for even five minutes he'd seen how pathologically shy she was, which wouldn't be the worst thing but she was so desperately needy on top of it.

He felt another burst of anger. Her family had tricked him. That was all there was to it.

Add that to the fact that there'd been that problem at work the week before the wedding, and his life was a right bollocks all the way around. He'd been written up and given a formal warning which everyone knew was just an excuse to give him the sack. He'd had an incident with the company's receptionist a few months back—the receptionist!—and she'd complained to management. If it had been a year ago nobody would have even listened to her, but what with all the hashtagmetoo rubbish going on, he was very likely about to get struck off!

Unbelievable! Over a stupid receptionist!

Heat flushed through his body in resurgent anger when he remembered trying to cancel any bogus honeymoon plans, but his mother had informed him that it had all been arranged and he was stuck with it. Which was how he'd ended up in this god-awful dump with a racist chef and a waiter he was sure was spitting in his food.

Raj glowered at the thought of both men. What he wouldn't give to see either of them with a blade between his ribs.

What he wouldn't give to be the one to put it there.

Feeling the fury boil up inside him he reminded himself that it was *Aishwarya* who'd ruined this evening.

First she sleeps with my brother but even if she didn't she'd been a whiny, annoying mess since we arrived...and now this? She humiliates me by causing a public scene?

Both his parents had promised him that Aishwarya was meek and compliant and that there would be no drama in their marriage.

Well, what do you call this? he thought angrily, throwing down his napkin and standing up abruptly.

He would have a private and very severe word with the stupid cow and they would start this marriage off on the right foot.

Especially if that foot was planted firmly up her fat arse.

It was pretty clear to Grace that the young Indian man, who had just tossed down his napkin, was about to charge off after his wife when Max Fountainbleu crossed his path carrying a heavy tray and nearly collided with him.

The Indian man squawked and made a big show of brushing off his jacket as if Max had somehow spilled food on him although Grace couldn't see any evidence of that.

"*Je m'excuse*, Monsieur Patel," Max said, still balancing the tray of *boeuf bourguignon*.

Alys Chaix came in through the main door to the dining room, hesitated for just a moment, and then went immediately to where Max and Mr. Patel were.

"Is everything all right, Mr. Patel?" Alys said cheerfully, her smile spreading across her face but her eyes probing and troubled.

I wouldn't have her job for anything, Grace thought.

"No, it's bloody not all right!" Patel shouted. "This oaf nearly knocked me down!"

All of a sudden Grace became aware of raised voices. Turning her head she saw two people enter the dining room, both of them talking at once.

She instantly recognized the real Madame Toureille—the stunning Hermès scarf was still knotted at her throat—followed by the man who had been with the single woman earlier today.

"Manon, *please*," Serge Toureille implored. "This is a family hotel!"

"Tell that to the whore you booked a room with!" Madame Toureille said, striding toward the lone woman with the book. Instantly Alys turned and ran to put herself between Madame Toureille and the single woman.

"Madame Toureille, I beg you," Alys said. "Do not do this."

"I want that whore out of here this instant," Madame Toureille said.

"I have a right to be here," the woman with the book said indignantly.

Madame Toureille's mouth fell open and she turned to her husband. "She's *English*?" she said in astonishment.

"Manon, please, stop for just one moment," Serge said.

"This ought to be good," Grace said in a whisper to Maggie who laughed in spite of herself.

"Does your slut know you're virtually penniless?" Manon said, bristling, her arms crossed. "And that all your money is mine?"

"Lisa, ignore her!" Serge called to the single woman who then slammed her book shut with a loud thump and stood up, her eyes flashing.

"If that woman dares to touch me, I shall sue this establishment!" Lisa shrieked at Alys. "Get this horrible creature out of my face this instant!"

"This hotel is no better than a brothel!" Madame Toureille shouted as Monsieur Toureille scurried around her to stand by Lisa.

"Madame Toureille, *please!*" Alys implored. "This is neither the time nor the place."

Madame Toureille let out a long frustrated scream and then pushed Alys hard just as Max walked by with the tray of *boeuf bourguignon.*

13

GOOD GOES THE BYE

M aggie saw the moment the *boeuf bourguignon* went airborne.

She swiveled away from the flying crockery as Max shouted and the tray of dishes and platters went flying. Alys landed on the floor and struggled to get up as Max fought not to step on her.

Max stood in the middle of the devastation, the front of his apron stained dark with sauce and no fewer than four plates of beef, potatoes and carrots dripping from the backs of chairs and onto the Oriental rug.

Manon stood staring at the destruction all around her, but rather than react apologetically to the havoc she'd caused, she turned to Alys whom Max had just helped back to her feet.

And slapped Alys across the face.

Maggie didn't remember jumping to her feet. If she'd thought about it she'd have realized that she should let Max handle it. But she didn't think. The only thing she saw was a brutal, antagonistic lunatic taking advantage of an employee just trying to do her job who was also a single mother.

Maggie didn't get as far as a single step from the table before Grace grabbed her hand.

"Maggie, no," she said. "Stay out of it."

It was exactly the sort of thing Laurent would have said. But because it was Grace and because Maggie was so irate by what Manon did, she flung Grace's hand off and turned on her.

"Is that your answer for everything, Grace?" Maggie said, her eyes narrowing as she glared at Grace. "Because *some* people actually want to try to help."

The stunned, hurt look on Grace's face stopped Maggie and she felt the blood drain from her cheeks.

At that moment Maggie knew she couldn't have strangled a puppy and felt any worse.

She turned away from the wounded expression on Grace's face.

Grace took the blow and let the insult hit its mark. After all, she deserved it. She deserved every awful word out of Maggie's mouth. Even so, she slumped back in her chair as if the air had been knocked out of her when Maggie turned away.

Across the room, the doors to the kitchen swung open and Chef Le Fleur appeared. Even from this distance Grace could see the glistening dome of the molded flan and in a flash Grace wanted to be ill.

Grace saw the chef hesitate in the door and then go back into the kitchen as if he'd forgotten something. She watched him disappear and thought, *thank God*. The flan could only be seen by Maggie as the pathetic attempt to make amends that it was.

How could a stupid custard even begin to fix the things I've done?

She'd been an idiot to think it could. She'd been an idiot to think any part of this whole stupid trip would do anything but underscore to Maggie what a useless excuse for a friend Grace was.

Grace looked down at her plate and tried to remember if there was a train leaving in the morning. There was no point in continuing this. It was just agony for both of them. As she stared at her plate, her vision blurry with tears, she saw the salt and pepper shaker begin to vibrate and then dance across the table.

Earthquake? she thought in bewilderment and looked around the room.

"Avalanche!" Max screamed as a sudden and terrible roar rocked the room, killing the light.

14

ONE FOR THE MONEY

The roar before the wall of snow crashed down upon them was something Maggie would never forget.

It drowned out all else—all sense, all thought, all perspective.

Max's one shouted word *Avalanche!* rang in Maggie's brain as the wall of snow smashed against the window of the dining room and extinguished the light.

The sound itself was a low rumbling that grew louder and louder until it was all there was to hear, a deafening barrage of noise that then ended abruptly and completely.

"Grace!" Maggie said when it was over. She'd been thrown to the floor, their table knocked over. But she was unhurt. "Grace! Are you okay?"

"I'm okay," Grace said breathlessly. "You?"

Before Maggie could answer she heard the others in the room. Weeping, calling for help.

"Madame Chaix!" Maggie called as she groped for her purse on the floor. "Can you answer me?"

"*Oui*! I am here," Alys said shakily.

"We need lights to find out who's hurt," Maggie called. "Where are the flashlights?"

Suddenly a sonorous crunching sound of falling rock and ice rippled through the room—like the roof was caving in and breaking away. Terrified screams followed.

"Everybody stay calm!" Detective Thompson shouted. "We need flashlights to see what we're up against!"

Maggie took in several long breaths to calm herself. She found her purse and felt inside for her cellphone. On her knees, she turned to look in the direction of the door that led to the lobby but all she could see was darkness. There should be a shaft of moonlight from the front of the hotel, she thought.

Unless the way is blocked.

Another slow ungodly creaking sound overhead prompted more screams and shot a tremor of dread up Maggie's spine. She realized the room had gone cold.

She turned on her cellphone but wasn't surprised to see the *No Service* message. She flipped on the flashlight function and saw that Detective Thompson had done the same thing. He looked flustered, his face thick with perspiration, his eyes darting around the room.

Maggie pulled herself to her feet and turned toward where the entrance to the dining room should have been. She took four tentative steps, bumping into tipped over tables and chairs before she reached the spot that should have been the door to the lobby.

Instead she found a giant pile of fallen debris from the beams and ceiling. The shattered crystal chandelier underfoot was in a thousand pieces of jagged glass, each one enough to seriously wound. The baby grand piano that she'd seen earlier in the lobby was on its side and blocking the entrance to the dining room.

Maggie put her hand to her mouth. Her heart was pounding in her throat and for a minute she felt like she couldn't breathe.

"Maggie?" Grace called.

We're trapped, Maggie thought with building panic, her fingers tingling. She turned and swept the room with the beam of her flashlight. The light wasn't strong enough to reach very far. She saw people moving. But there were no other lights.

Thompson was talking loudly, urging people to use their cellphone lights and to stay calm.

"Help me!" Lisa called out. "Serge, help me! I'm hurt!"

Avoiding the thousands of shards of broken crystal on the carpet, Maggie picked her way carefully back to the table. She touched Grace's shoulder to tell her she was there.

The appearance of a stronger beam of light made Maggie turn to see Alys standing in the center of the dining room. Maggie's heart nearly stopped when Alys played the flashlight beam along the walls of the dining room and Maggie was able to see the extent of the destruction. The dining room ceiling beams were broken and jutting downward with the ceiling tenuously still aloft. The fractured beams held up the bulk of the ceiling but head clearance was no more than around six feet.

In some places much less.

The plate glass window that faced the mountain showed only darkness where moments before had been the tail end of a dying sunset. The dark barricade of snow pressed against the glass. She could hear the frightening intermittent subtle creaks as the window glass continued to crack like breaking ice on the surface of a frozen lake.

Serge Tourielle knelt beside his English girlfriend who was moaning.

"Give me the torch!" the young Indian man shouted knocking furniture out of the way to get to Alys. "My wife is trapped in the loo!"

Maggie could hear a faint voice crying from down the hall where the restrooms were.

"No, you don't, boyo!" Thompson snarled moving clumsily to intercept Patel's reach for Alys's flashlight.

"Give it to him!" Maggie commanded. "His wife may be hurt."

Patel snatched the flashlight from Alys plunging the room once more into darkness and dashed down the hall.

Maggie saw that her cellphone battery was low. She had intended to charge it later tonight.

"There's another set of torches in the kitchen," Max's voice said from the middle of the room. He sounded unsure and afraid.

No one made a motion to move and within seconds Patel was back, leading his stunned wife over to the group. Maggie used the now faint beam of her cellphone to pick her way to them and took the heavy flashlight from him.

"Max," she called over her shoulder, "come with me and show me where the other flashlights are."

"I will go with you," Serge said, climbing quickly to his feet.

"That is unnecessary, Monsieur Tourielle," Maggie said, and turned toward the kitchen with the flashlight. "Max knows the layout better."

"I'm in charge," Thompson said, not moving from where he stood next to Grace. "I should be the one to go."

Maggie felt a surge of fury at this pompous little man who would prefer to debate rank rather than just get the job done. But she bit her tongue and gestured for Max to lead the way to the kitchen.

The kitchen was a catastrophe. Like the dining room, most of its ceiling was sagging into the center of the room. Maggie played the beam of her flashlight around the room. Only a small section of the room would allow an average-sized man to stand upright. The stove, ovens and most of the sinks were all squashed like accordions under the weight of the slumping ceiling.

"In here," Max said, moving to a pantry closet and tugging on the door. It was stuck.

"Careful," Maggie said. "We don't want the rest of the roof to go." She pointed her beam at the ceiling. "The top of the pantry is touching the ceiling."

Maggie thought she could hear something dripping across

the room but the space was too badly damaged to allow passage through. "Where is the chef?" she asked.

"Chef!" Max called. He turned to Maggie. "Perhaps he is in the WC. There is access to the restrooms from the kitchen."

"Can you check for me, please?" Maggie asked, handing him the flashlight. "I'll work on the pantry door."

She waited a moment for Max to walk bent over through the one section where the ceiling hadn't fallen and then disappear through a narrow ingress off the kitchen. Without the flashlight, she was in total darkness. She'd left her cellphone on one of the tables back in the dining room.

She put both hands on the pantry door, running her fingers up and down it to see if it was broken before gently trying to ease it open. She heard a long groaning sound of metal against metal and she held her breath.

Was the ceiling about to give way? Should they all just stay put and not move?

Maggie took in a long breath and fought the feeling of panic that was welling up in her chest. There was nothing she could do about whether the ceiling was about to fall. She focused on trying to ease the pantry door open by millimeters. It creaked and suddenly gave away in her hands. She immediately let go, afraid she'd gone too far.

After a second of holding her breath, she inched the door open wider. Without the flashlight she couldn't see what was inside but she moved her hands to the first shelf and felt cans of food. She was on the third shelf by the time Max came back stepping slowly across the kitchen floor strewn with pots and small appliances.

"He's not there," he said. He shined his light into the pantry. There in front were four flashlights and two battery-operated lanterns.

"Pray the batteries are still good," Maggie said as she pulled them out.

"LeFleur keeps them up to date," Max said.

"I assume he has a first-aid kit in here somewhere too?"

Max reached over her head and pulled out a box with a small red cross on it. A bulky plastic container of metal measuring cups fell from the overhead shelf, hitting Maggie on the shoulder. Pain shot through her in an electrifying jolt and she grabbed the pantry door to steady herself.

"*Je suis désolé*," Max said.

"Never mind," Maggie said between gritted teeth. She released the door to rub her aching shoulder where the container had hit.

"Can you take the first-aid kit and the two lanterns into the dining room to see who's hurt?" she asked.

He nodded and quickly turned to make his way out of the kitchen. Maggie flashed her light beam beyond the pantry where the main prep table was. It didn't make sense that the chef wasn't here. He wouldn't leave his kitchen in the middle of dinner! Where the hell was he?

She played the beam along the floor slowly, fighting the urge to leave the kitchen and get back to the relative sanctuary in the dining room. But something kept her there. Something made her stay just a few moments longer.

When Maggie finally found what she'd been looking for, she wasn't at all surprised.

There, under the prep table...

...was a body broken and covered in blood.

15

DAMNED IF YOU DO

T he day after their visit to the village broke cold and gray at Domaine St-Buvard. As usual, Laurent was the first one up. Normally, after making coffee he'd putter around in his kitchen—except for his vineyard his favorite place in the world—until everyone else began to drift in when he would make *pain perdu* or *frittatas*.

This morning, he didn't feel like cooking. That in itself should have told him that something was wrong. Instead of examining why he felt that way, he took his coffee, pulled on a heavy topcoat and stepped out onto the terrace.

A squadron of olive and fig trees lined a pebbled path from the terrace leading to the fields. At the threshold of the fields, the oaks and cypress trees bunched together to create a virtual park, framing his forty hectares of grape fields and at the same time outlining the boundaries of the property.

From where Laurent stood he could see patchy brown grass peeking out from the snow that bordered the terrace. The sun was struggling to make an appearance but if today was anything like yesterday, it would fail.

Laurent drank his hot, very black coffee and scanned the lines of his vineyard as he had done so many times over the years. He knew and loved every hillock, every line, every curve and dip of the fields. He knew the rows intimately. He'd personally planted, pruned, weeded and harvested every inch of this land. As he gazed at the fields he waited for the feeling of fulfillment and satisfaction that the habit usually brought with it.

Not this time.

He looked beyond the horizon of his fields in the direction of Jean-Luc's property. If he were to buy Jean-Luc's fields—putting an end to two hundred years of Alexandre ownership of the land in this area—he would own far beyond what he could see from one vantage point. And if Eduard's property could be made viable again—even further.

Is that what he wanted? Did he want *more* land while he was already wrestling with what to do about his own?

The bite of the cold air seemed to drill down his collar and he shivered and set down his coffee mug on one of the wrought iron tables on the terrace. He turned to glance back at the *mas*. There were no lights or movement from within.

Zouzou would sleep late, as would both Jemmy and Mila. Normally Elspeth would be up but Laurent guessed she was delaying her entrance in order to supervise John.

Last night, the man had thrown a board game at the wall, sending Maggie's little dog Petit-Four squirming under the couch.

And Elspeth thinks having Maggie home will help this?

But Laurent knew that Elspeth wasn't counting on Maggie's expertise in dealing with Alzheimer's. She wanted support. A friend. To not be alone in this.

Laurent turned and walked down the terrace toward the shed that marked the end of the garden and the beginning of the vineyard. The structure had burned to the ground eight months before—arson done by a friend of Grace's—and had been designed and rebuilt to blend in with the landscape.

He walked past an ancient hut with an abandoned well in

front. He and Maggie often walked this way after dinner when the final rays of sunlight draped the vineyard in a soft glow.

He turned back to the shed and was still twenty yards away when he saw that the lock on the door was laying on the ground. He instantly remembered Jean-Luc mentioning he'd had some tools stolen from his garage recently. Laurent cursed the fact that he'd not gotten around to replacing his big dogs. They would have raised the alarm if someone had been on the property in the night.

Entering the shed, Laurent saw that his shelves of nails and screws were disrupted. He determined quickly that nothing had been taken. That made him frown.

Why break in if not to steal?

He straightened the shelves and scooped up loose screws and nails back into their wooden bowls.

Vandalism. Not theft. That meant kids.

There was nothing of value in this shed. There was only the thrill of breaking into it to leave evidence that you did it.

He ran over the possibilities from the village. There were very few young people in St-Buvard. Anyone who could, left the area immediately. As for teenagers, there were only girls around here that Laurent could think of.

And girls don't do this.

Sighing, he spent the next twenty minutes repairing and reat-taching the lock. As he did, his thoughts went back to Maggie. Last night he'd tried calling her again using Elspeth's phone since he had still yet to locate his own. The call had gone straight to voice mail.

He had to assume that Maggie was busy sorting things out with Grace in long intense periods of talk interspersed with hours of skiing. She deserved this break. It had been a hard autumn for her in many ways and with his burgeoning concern about the vineyard and what he was doing with it, he hadn't been the best of company. Plus, regardless of what she said, it was good for Maggie to finally connect again with Grace.

Satisfied with his work on the repaired lock, he turned back to the house, sure that everyone would be up by now. What with the effect that Zouzou had had on Jemmy, Laurent had recently had to eliminate television and all access to electronics. Even at seven years old, Jemmy was addicted to them and Laurent had to admit it was nice to have a quiet house again instead of twenty-four seven news or children's shows. It occurred to him that he might suggest this to Maggie as a pleasant change one day a week.

As he approached the house, he saw the French doors were opened onto the terrace and Elspeth stood outside, holding her cardigan tight around her, obviously waiting for him.

Merde. Now what?

As he neared, he saw her face was pinched with fear.

Laurent's first thought was John. He'd fallen or hurt himself. But Elspeth allayed that notion immediately.

"It's Zouzou," Elspeth said, her breath making puffs of dense fog in the cold air. "She's missing."

16

LOST IN THE DARKNESS

What could be taking them so long in the kitchen? Serge wondered. He tried to consider the fact that it was dark in there and they were focused on finding lanterns.

"Serge?" Lisa said in a small voice. "Can you find me something to wrap up in? I'm so cold."

"Of course, *chérie*," Serge said, patting her shoulder although he couldn't help but think that sitting on the floor was not the warmest option available.

He twisted out of his jacket and draped it over her shoulders. When he did he noticed she looked very pale even given the circumstances.

"*Chérie*?" he asked, squatting by her. "You are ill?"

"No, no, I'm fine," Lisa said. "Did you get things sorted out with your wife? Because I must say it rather looked as if you hadn't."

Serge blew out an impatient breath and turned to look at Manon. She was sitting at Lisa's table, both hands gripping the tablecloth and staring at him. Her eyes narrowed to slits of loathing.

Incredible! We are in the middle of a life and death situation and all she has in her heart is how much she detests me.

He turned and slipped his arms under Lisa's legs, pulling her up into his arms.

"Serge, no!" Lisa said, yelping in pain. "What are you doing?"

He stood with her in his arms well aware from the hissing intake of breath from Manon as she watched them.

"I am moving you away from the window," he said. "The glass could break at any moment."

Carefully, Serge inched his way toward the table where the two American women had been sitting—as far away from the window as possible. He knew that when the one called Maggie returned she would undoubtedly go to where her friend was. If there was going to be fallout as a result of any surprising discoveries in the kitchen, he would do well to be close when it happened to mitigate damages.

Why couldn't he have gone with her? It would have made everything so much easier.

Lisa let out a small groan and Serge took the opportunity to rest for a moment, leaning a hip against one of the tables.

"How are you hurt, *chérie*?" he said.

"It's my foot," Lisa said in a labored of breath. "Something fell on it when the...when the..."

"*Je sais*," he murmured, setting her down gently in one of the chairs that had been righted in the moments after the avalanche hit. "Let me look at it."

Lisa pushed him away with both hands. "Tell me why she's still here," she said, her face screwed into a visage of pain and fear.

Serge sighed but reached for Lisa's foot. He fumbled for his cellphone and directed the light onto her foot.

The gash was bloody and looked painful. Serge couldn't tell how deep it was. He turned to look at the blonde American sitting at the table.

"Do you have acetaminophen?" he asked. "Or aspirin?"

"Yes, I think so." She dug into her purse and pulled out a small bottle of pills and handed it to Thompson who handed it to Serge.

Serge poured a glass of water on the table and shook out four pills into his hand.

"Your friend has been gone a long time," he said to Grace as he handed the pills and the glass to Lisa. "Perhaps I should go see if they need help?"

"I think you've got your hands full right where you are, mate," Thompson said gruffly. "In fact, the less everybody moves the better."

As if his own words had spurred him, the burly Englishman suddenly stood up and spoke loudly to everyone in the room.

"Oy! Listen up!" he said. "There's as yet no need to panic so we'll all do better by staying put!"

Serge looked at Lisa who was wincing. Over her shoulder he could see Manon advancing on them and his stomach dropped.

"Oy! Madame!" Thompson bellowed to Manon. "*Restez*-where you are, *s'il vous plait*. It's bloody dangerous to be walking about right now!"

Ignoring the detective, Manon turned to confront Serge, her face hollow-eyed with fury.

"Really, Serge?" she said in French. "You would give up it all for this? She's *old*." She gestured to Lisa huddling under his coat on the chair in front of them.

"What's she saying?" Lisa said. She spoke French poorly and understood it even less.

"When we are out of this situation—" Serge began.

"You will be a pauper!" Manon snarled. "I will take it all from you! The children, the house!"

"Madame," Thompson said loudly. "If you would kindly lower your voice."

Manon took another step closer to Serge and Lisa. "Is she worth losing all of it, Serge?"

"Serge?" Lisa said. "What is she saying?"

Serge rubbed a hand over his face, gulping down quick breaths to try and calm himself.

"They are coming back!" the concierge, Alys said excitedly.

Serge turned to look toward the kitchen, his eyes desperately searching Maggie and Max's faces and then their hands as they approached, his stomach lurching in dread and expectation.

Just watching Serge mewl over that English bitch made Manon want to walk over there and stab him in the neck with a steak knife. He kept looking over at her so Manon wasn't fooled by thinking he did it for any other reason than to make her jealous. But even knowing that didn't help.

She could never take him back now. No matter how he begged or pleaded with her to reconsider. Now the only thing she could do was make sure that every waking minute of the rest of his life was a living nightmare.

If she was able to let him live that long.

When she thought of all those years when she'd supported the family while Serge spent his time trying to write his ridiculous science fiction novels it was all she could do to sit still in her chair. Did he really think that's how this was going to play out?

Did he know her at all?

She watched Serge as he rearranged the tablecloth over his whore's shoulders and felt a stab of fury.

He could do this after what happened to me at the hospital? she thought savagely. *After ten years of working every shift, swallowing every insult, I am dismissed for unprofessional conduct? And Serge's response is to take an English whore?*

She felt her muscles literally quivering in rage as she worked to calm herself.

The ski instructor cleared his throat noisily and she glanced at him where he stood next to the little concierge, his arm protectively around her. Every once in awhile the man would look over nervously at Manon.

What did the idiot think? That she was so unbalanced that she would reveal to the whole ensemble what had happened between the two of them last night in the linen closet?

She snorted derisively. He could relax. He'd not looked so bad at one in the morning in a darkened hallway after a bottle of French single malt. But the bright light of day could be cruel.

Did the oaf really think she'd reveal to Serge that she'd been so desperate for pay back that she screwed the octogenarian ski instructor? She shivered in humiliation.

No worries, Monsieur! I would rather bury this knife in your chest than let the world know to what depths Serge's betrayal has driven me.

She directed her attention to the Englishwoman who was now staring arrogantly at her.

On the other hand it would be good to let Serge know that he wasn't the only one who could step outside the marriage. What did he think? That I am only here to pay the rent and develop stretch marks from bearing his children?

"Manon," Serge said, "quit staring at Lisa. You are making us both uncomfortable."

Manon bared her teeth and stuck her chin out defiantly.

"Tell your whore I'll look where I like," Manon snarled.

Her fingers unconsciously tightened around the handle of the steak knife she held under the table.

17

A MIDNIGHT DREARY

L aurent walked past Elspeth to the salon. The fire was out in the hearth and he felt the chill of the house sink into his bones. Jemmy, Mila and John sat at the kitchen counter, watching him. John was wearing mismatched socks and stared in confusion at his surroundings.

"I sent Jemmy up to get her for breakfast," Elspeth said, breathlessly. "Her bed doesn't look like it's been slept in. Unless she's in the habit of making it when she gets up?"

Laurent snorted, and rubbed a hand across the back of his neck, trying to concentrate.

He ran the memory tapes in his mind to remember the last time he'd seen the girl. As usual, she'd caused a problem around dinnertime and as usual, he'd asked her to remove herself from the dinner table.

There hadn't seemed much point in going up to talk with her. She'd made it clear that she either wouldn't speak or she'd give herself an opportunity to sass Laurent. Neither were situations he felt in any hurry to provoke.

But he should have gone up anyway.

You can't just send someone to their room and forget about them. As much as you may want to.

"Do you have your cellphone?" Laurent asked Elspeth. She hurried to her purse where it sat on the couch. "Jemmy and Mila, did Zouzou tell you where she was going?"

"No, Papa," they both replied.

Elspeth handed Laurent her phone. "I feel just terrible about this."

Laurent shoved the phone in his coat pocket. "Does John still have a phone?"

Elspeth nodded.

"*Bon*," he said as he snatched the car keys from the hook by the front door. "I will call when I find her. Meanwhile keep the children inside until I return."

He was gone before she could respond.

Laurent sped down the road leading to Jean-Luc and Danielle's place. It seemed unlikely that Zouzou would walk the two miles there in the cold but she had reacted positively to Danielle the other day and if the child wanted to run away, Laurent could think of no place more likely.

He pulled to a screeching halt in the circular drive in front of the old farmhouse, spraying gravel in a wide arc as he did. It was true he could have called first—probably should have—but he was sure Zouzou was here and he was eager to confront her face to face and without warning.

Danielle opened the door in her bathrobe, her eyes wide with concern. As soon as Laurent saw her, he knew he'd been wrong. Zouzou wasn't here.

"We have misplaced Zouzou," he said apologetically, silently cursing himself, for he knew Danielle would worry now. "It's not a problem," he said as he turned back to his car.

"Laurent!" Danielle called as he maneuvered the car around the circular drive and headed back to the main road. "Please call when you find her!"

He gave an abrupt toot on the horn and raced down the driveway, his mind trying to think where the child could have gone.

Has she really left last night? Has she been out all night? But where? Where could she find a bed for the night?

His stomach churning, he paused at the end of Danielle's driveway to ponder which way to go. Back to the left would allow him to scour the vineyard on foot, except it was not believable that the girl had spent the night on the frozen ground of the vineyard with her warm bed not a hundred yards away. To his right was the village. In frustration and without any better idea, Laurent turned the car in that direction.

He drove well over the speed limit on the winding road up a steep incline which was thrown into deep morning shade by the sycamores that lined the road.

Why would she leave? What was the matter with her? He glanced at Elspeth's cellphone on the passenger seat next to him. He wasn't tempted to call Grace—not yet anyway. This matter would be resolved within the hour, and there was no point in upsetting Grace in the meantime. But perhaps a call to Windsor? To at least find out what he had left out of his description of Zouzou's unhappiness?

An eleven year old child so bitterly unhappy that she runs away in the middle of a winter night? Surely Windsor must know more about why Zouzou was so unhappy?

Laurent reached the village and parked the car on the curb in front of the shuttered bistro, noting that the *For Sale* sign had slipped in the window and was now practically unnoticeable in its current position. This early in the morning, the village was quiet. Le Canard would be open for coffee but except for the proprietor there would likely be nobody inside.

Laurent crossed the street to the square that fronted the café bar. Theroux had seen him approach and stood in the doorway.

"What is wrong?" Theroux said, instantly picking up that Laurent was not here for a leisurely morning coffee.

"Have you seen the American girl staying with us?" Laurent held out a hand to indicate her height. "Blonde."

"The fat one? *Non*, sorry. Not since you were here day before yesterday."

Laurent turned away in frustration, his hands on his hips, and tried to think. Theroux stood silently in the doorway, waiting.

Laurent retraced their steps that day in his mind. He had come to Le Canard and Zouzou and Jemmy had wandered the village. Suddenly he turned back to Theroux.

"I saw a young girl in the village," he said. "She looked homeless. Not from one of the village families."

Theroux nodded. "*Ah, oui. La gitane.*" *The gypsy.*

Gypsies often came through the area but they never stayed long. Usually they were here for seasonal work to help harvest the grapes. It was not at all usual for them to be here in the dead of winter.

"Do you know where her people are staying?"

"*Non*, sorry. Only the usual places."

Laurent knew those places. Under bridges, beside abandoned crofts, in the fields just outside the village limits—any place they could park their caravans in order to better pollute the area with their refuse and noise.

Thanking Theroux, Laurent hurried back to his car.

The rest of the morning Laurent drove a careful radius of twenty kilometers around the village. He went to every bridge and vacant field but there was no sign of any gypsies. At one point, as his car idled in the middle of a country road as he tried to decide where to go next, he saw an old man emerge from the woods with his dog.

The man was easily in his seventies and bent over but his

pace was sure and brisk. Laurent switched off the ignition and got out of the car.

"Excuse me, Monsieur," Laurent called. "Have you seen any gypsies in this area?"

The man frowned and looked around.

"Not the time of year for gypsies," he said. "If you want to find gypsies, you must go to Spain."

Laurent felt a splinter of discouragement. This old fellow lived in the area. If he hadn't heard of any gypsies around here, there likely were none. The presence of gypsies—had there been any—would have ranked as an immediate and prevalent topic of conversation to anyone living in the environs.

Theroux had been wrong.

And Laurent was wasting valuable time.

After thanking the old man, Laurent returned to his car and drove slowly back to the village, his eyes on the woods and the fields that bordered the roads on the possible chance of a miracle that Zouzou might be in the woods. Again, to have spent the night outdoors in this weather was unimaginable—for anyone, let alone an eleven year old girl not used to roughing it.

This was his fault, of course. He had not dealt with Zouzou, he had shelved her. He felt a flush of heat race through his body.

He called Domaine St-Buvard and Elspeth immediately picked up.

"Have you found her?" she asked breathlessly, dashing any hopes that Laurent had that the girl had found her way back home.

"*Non*," Laurent said. "But I have a few other places to look. Could you put Jemmy on?"

Laurent drove to the entrance of the village as he waited for his son to come to the phone.

"*Oui*, Papa?" Jemmy said breathlessly. Laurent could well imagine that Zouzou's disappearance was a cause for much excitement for both children.

"When you and Zouzou were in the village the other day, she talked to a strange girl. Did you see her?"

"*Oui*, Papa. Gizelle."

"Who are Gizelle's parents, do you know?"

"*Non*, Papa. I think she is an orphan."

Lately Jemmy had been reading Lemony Snickett and in his mind he now saw everyone as an orphan.

"Do you know her last name?"

"*Non*, Papa."

"Do you know where she lives?"

"Oh, *oui*! She lives at the old monastery, she said. On rue Vincent."

Laurent was already turning the car around as Jemmy spoke. He felt his pulse quicken as he considered the likelihood that Zouzou was at the monastery.

Unless this was another dead end, if it was true that Zouzou had somehow gotten to the monastery—easily four miles away—and she was there and safe he vowed that he'd get to the bottom of why she was so unhappy—after he throttled her.

18

THE SOUND OF ALL HELL BREAKING LOOSE

By the time Maggie rejoined the others in the dining room, there were two lanterns glowing on two tables. Everyone was crowded around Grace and Maggie's table. It was the furthest point from the window which was undoubtedly the least safe spot in the dining room. The area by the window was where the snow wanted in, the spot that would be consumed first.

Maggie hurried over to where Grace sat, hugging her arms, a tablecloth wrapped around her shoulders as the temperature in the room continued to drop by the minute. There was an enormous expanse of black where the wall of snow outside the window stood like an ominous threat.

Could the glass—cracking more every few moments now and each time louder—hold out? Would the dining room fill with suffocating snow as soon as it did?

The young Indian woman sat shivering in her thin sweater and pashmina at the table beside Grace's. Her husband stood by, oblivious to her discomfort, his arms crossed on his chest as he glared alternately at Thompson and Max.

"Everyone! We need to stay together!" the Englishman bellowed.

Maggie seriously worried that the volume of his voice might dislodge what appeared to be precariously placed beams in the half-fallen ceiling above them.

She glanced up nervously and shined her flashlight along the ceiling. It was low with jagged pieces of beams revealing how the supports beneath it had snapped under the pressure and weight of the avalanche. Was it lower than it had been a few moments earlier?

"*Ecoutez, tout le monde!*" Alys cried out frantically. She was standing next to Max, wringing her hands "Please to stay calm!" she said.

"Yes," Thompson shouted. "Everyone stay calm!"

His voice—laced with panic and fear—seemed to have the opposite effect on the people huddled by the table.

"Madame?" Serge said, licking his lips. "Is...is everything okay?"

Maggie noticed that Serge had settled Lisa in the chair that Maggie had sat in at dinner. But his eyes were on Maggie.

And he looked nervous.

The Englishwoman looked pale. Her eyes were large and terrified. She was sweating heavily. Serge had draped his suit jacket over her shoulders.

Before Maggie could answer Serge, Manon Toureille addressed Alys in a strident voice.

"None of our phones are working!" she said. "What are your emergency procedures for emergencies like this? I demand to know what's being done!"

"Everyone should stay calm," Thompson said again and it was all Maggie could do not to tell him to shut up. She didn't want to upset anyone more than they already were, but she felt she should tell someone about the chef. And for that, self-imposed or

not, Thompson appeared to be the closest semblance of
authority.

"Detective Thompson," Maggie said firmly, resisting the urge
to pull him away from his place in front of the group.

He turned to her and put his hand on her shoulder. "Just stay
calm," he said, his voice strident, his eyes blinking rapidly.

"I *am* calm. We need to find blankets to help everyone stay
warm. We don't know how long it will be before they can dig us
out."

And I need to tell you that there's a dead body in the other room.

"What are you saying?" Mr. Patel said, pushing his wife aside
to confront Maggie and Thompson. "Do you have information
about the rescuers? Do you know something?"

Up close, Maggie was able to see that Raj Patel was really
quite young. She and Grace had guessed that he and Mrs. Patel
were newlyweds and that had been confirmed by Alys during the
afternoon *apéro.*

"Mr. Patel is it?" Maggie said. "I am Maggie Dernier. This is
Detective Thompson."

"He don't need to know me name," Thompson snarled.

Maggie felt her body tense.

"Oh, why is that then?" Patel said, stepping up to Thompson.
A vein twitched in his forehead. "Because I'm Indian?"

"Stop it!" Maggie said, putting her hand on Patel's chest and
pressing hard. "We have a problem here and this isn't helping!
Please, Mr. Patel, step back."

Patel looked Maggie up and down and she guessed he was
not accustomed to taking orders from women.

"Sod off," he said to Maggie.

Max Fountainbleu gave Patel a hard push, knocking the
younger man backwards onto a nearby table.

"Behave, Monsieur!" Max said, holding up a threatening
finger to the young man.

"I have this handled!" Thompson said heatedly to Max. He

was gripping his stomach as if he were in pain. Maggie had just about enough of blustering men. She turned to Alys.

"Is there any another way out of the dining room other than the doors leading to the lobby?" Maggie asked.

Alys shook her head, her eyes going to the barricade of sagging ceiling beams and debris that blocked that avenue. "*Non,*" she said softly.

"Okay," Maggie said. "I think all of us being quiet is the most important thing we can do at this stage. We need to be able to hear the rescuers as they try to reach us."

"*Non!*" Manon said imperiously. "That is wrong. We must make as much noise as possible so that they know where we are!"

"But won't noise bring the ceiling down?" Grace asked nervously, looking up.

"Is the ceiling going to fall more?" Mrs. Patel asked, biting her lip.

Maggie turned to Patel who was straightening his clothes in short jerking motions as if trying to compose himself after his altercation with Max.

"Mr. Patel," Maggie said. "Can you tell us the condition of the restrooms?"

"The men's restroom is buggered," he said sullenly. "But the women's is still intact."

Maggie turned to Alys. "How many stalls?"

Alys frowned as if she didn't understand.

"It is one room with a toilet," Aishwarya Patel said softly.

Maggie smiled encouragingly at her. "Thank you." She turned to address the others. "The kitchen is badly damaged and water is leaking from somewhere. From what I could see of the ceiling I'd say it's even more unstable than where we are right now."

"Unstable?" Serge said worriedly.

"She means unsafe," Lisa said to him with a quivering bottom lip.

"And it's safe *here*?" Manon said.

Thompson grunted and sat down heavily as if his legs had given out from under him.

"We have light," he said, panting. "And I am sure they are working to rescue us as we speak."

Relieved that Thompson appeared to be calming down instead of upsetting everyone, Maggie turned to Lisa.

"Can I ask how badly you are hurt?" she asked. She couldn't help but notice that the woman appeared to be perspiring heavily. And it was cold in the dining room.

"I'm fine," Lisa said. "Something hit my foot and I can't put any weight on it."

Maggie looked around the room. "Does anybody here have any first aid training?"

Alys walked over to Lisa. "I know a little," she said.

"I'm fine," Lisa said stoically, her face clenched in pain.

"My wife is a doctor," Serge said.

All eyes turned to Manon who stood watching Lisa with her arms crossed. Maggie didn't know what kind of oath French doctors took in their profession but if it was anything like American doctors, she was clearly willing to circumvent it.

"You are a doctor?" Maggie asked her.

"I am not going to touch that pig," Manon said.

"No one would expect you to," Grace said. "But as soon as we are rescued I for one will report you to whatever professional board you work under for failing to help an injured woman. Is your English good enough to understand me, Madame?"

Manon glared at Grace and then stalked over to where Lisa sat.

Lisa clutched at Serge's arm. "Do not let her touch me!" she screamed.

Manon turned back to Grace and said smugly, "The patient has refused treatment."

Already feeling exhausted and cold, Maggie looked at Max and spoke in a low voice.

"Monsieur Fountainbleu would you be so kind as to escort Detective Thompson to the kitchen to see something I found there?"

"Eh?" Thompson said. "Can't you just tell me? I've got a belly ache that won't quit."

"I'd prefer you see it for yourself," Maggie said, wanting nothing more than to slap the man into stepping up.

"Well, I'd prefer not to have to go into an area that you've already said is clearly unsafe," Thompson said.

Maggie noticed that the others had retreated into separate groupings and were talking among themselves.

"Fine," she said, dropping her voice and addressing Thompson directly. "I found Chef LeFleur's body when I was there a few moments ago."

Grace gasped audibly forcing everyone else to look in her direction. Immediately, Grace pretended to succumb to a coughing attack and the Patels and the Toureilles turned away.

"*Oh, mon Dieu,*" Max said, in a low voice and shaking his head. "I am being afraid of this."

"Can you go look at the body?" Maggie said to Thompson. "I'm ninety-nine percent sure he's dead but if he isn't—"

"What is it?" Serge said. "You have found something? What have you found?"

"It's nothing to worry about," Maggie said. "It's just something I want to clear up with Detective Thompson here."

Serge looked at Thompson. "You are the police?" he asked, blanching.

But before Thompson could reply Lisa reached over to pull Serge back to her.

"Please don't leave me," she said. "I need you, Serge."

Serge gave one last hesitant look at Maggie and Thompson and then turned back to sit next to Lisa.

"I'll go," Thompson muttered, still gripping his stomach. "But since you know where the body is, Mrs. Derne-yur, you should come with me."

"*C'est ridicule!*" Max said. "I will go."

"No, he's right," Maggie said. "Meanwhile Max, can you and Madame Chaix gather up the tablecloths so we can use them to keep warm?"

She gave another quick, sympathetic smile to Mrs. Patel who was sitting in a chair and shivering, pulling her pashmina tightly around her. Maggie turned to follow Thompson in the direction of the kitchen.

As soon as they reached the kitchen, Thompson stopped. He shined his flashlight on the ceiling and refused to go another step.

"It's not safe," he said. "The bloke is dead. How could he not be?"

Maggie pushed past him and tiptoed to the pantry. The door was now open and swinging gently on its hinges. She shined her flashlight at the floor under the prep table where she'd seen the body.

Her stomach churned as she saw the illuminated form of the dead man on the floor. Nausea gripped her and she fought for control as the thought came to her that this man had been alive and vibrant not one hour before. She balked at going any nearer. But she knew she had to. She had to confirm that there was no hope for him. She couldn't live with herself if she didn't and found out later he'd been only injured.

"Do ye see him, Mrs. Derne-yer?" Thompson called and Maggie cringed. First for the way he mangled her last name but mostly for his volume that seemed to make the rafters creak and the dishes on the shelf tremble.

"Shut up," she said quietly over her shoulder, long past caring about anyone's ego. She forced herself not to touch anything— knowing that columns or walls that looked stable could easily be the piece that brought down the whole house of cards. She inched over to where the body was.

Her flashlight beam brought the body into sharp relief and she was relieved she wouldn't need to go any further to determine if he was dead or not.

He was clearly dead. He lay on his front but his head was twisted and his eyes were open and unseeing. There was a wide circle of blood pooled beneath this body.

And the handle of a Laguiole steak knife stuck out from the center of his back.

19

GOING DOWN HARD

At first Maggie couldn't understand what she was seeing. Her mind ran through the possibilities starting with the improbable image of a knife flying from a shelf during the avalanche and embedding in the chef's back.

Suddenly she felt too warm and a pulse tightened in her midsection.

"Mrs. Derne-yer?

Maggie took a tentative step backward, her hand grabbing the corner of the pantry for support. A loud shuddering creak shot through the kitchen.

"Be careful!" Thompson screamed.

Maggie felt an irresistible urge to turn and run—away from the body, away from the impending demolition of the room disintegrating around her, away from the triggering screeching of the man behind her.

She grabbed the swinging door of the pantry. It wouldn't support her but it helped steady her. She gripped the metal edge of the door so tightly it cut into the palm of her hand.

"Detective Thompson," she said, trying to hear herself over

the pounding of her accelerated heartbeat. "You must come here and confirm what I am seeing."

"Bloody hell, Missus—" the man started.

"Chef LeFleur has been stabbed to death," Maggie said between clenched teeth. "You must see for yourself." She turned to look at him. His mouth hung open in shock at her statement.

"Stabbed?" he said as if he didn't understand the word. "How in the—"

Maggie moved to where he stood. "Go confirm it," she said stiffly, "or I'll have Max do it."

As she expected, that's all it took. Thompson's face clenched in an expression of pain and determination.

"Where?" he asked as he moved ahead of her.

"Behind the pantry closet. Under the prep table."

Maggie walked carefully back to the entrance of the dining room. In spite of the cold, a layer of perspiration had formed on her face. Within seconds, Thompson was backing out of the kitchen.

"You saw him?" Maggie asked him.

"Yes. Stabbed in the back," he said, shaking his head in bewilderment.

"So *not* killed in the avalanche," Maggie said more to herself than to the detective. She turned to make her way back to the group. All eyes watched her and Thompson as they picked their way back to them.

Maggie's mind was whirling with a million discordant thoughts. Whoever stabbed the chef had used a steak knife which was on all the tables and which meant anyone had access. She tried to remember the last time she'd seen the chef. Max had been in and out of the kitchen of course but so had Patel.

Could the Indian have gone in, stabbed the chef and then come back to placidly sit at his table and await his dinner?

Maggie glanced at Patel. He didn't look particularly upset—or not any more upset than the rest of them. But he was a hot head.

There was no way he had the cool nerves to do such a thing and then go back to his table as if nothing had happened.

Serge on the other hand stood wringing his hands as he watched Maggie approach.

Almost like he knew what she had found.

"What is it?" Alys said as Maggie and Thompson rejoined the others. There was a stack of tablecloths on the table behind Alys. Lisa and Mrs. Patel had already wrapped themselves in several.

"Chef LeFleur is dead," Maggie said glancing first at Serge's face and then Raj's for any hint that one of them already knew this.

"*Non!*" Alys said, her voice thick with anguish. Maggie glanced at her. Had there been something between the concierge and the chef?

"How can this be?" Serge said too loudly.

"I *told* you the kitchen was unsafe!" Max said.

Maggie narrowed her eyes at him. Max was certainly the most obvious suspect. He had access and means. But did he have motive?

"He didn't die in the avalanche," Thompson said. "He was murdered."

The rest of the group gasped and immediately began to edge away from each other. It annoyed Maggie that Thompson would deliver the news like that—or at all. It was almost as if he *wanted* to upset everyone.

Suddenly tired, Maggie sat down next to Grace.

"Are you okay, darling?" Grace asked softly.

Maggie nodded but she felt numb.

"I remember the last time the chef was in the dining room," Grace said.

"You do? When?" Maggie twisted in her seat to look at Grace.

"I'd asked him to prepare a special dish for us. It's why we were seated at Table Six. I saw him about to come out with it and then he went back in. Like maybe he forgot something? He didn't come back out again. I don't remember how close that was to the avalanche hitting."

So that would have been *after* Patel had gone in, Maggie thought, putting *him* in the clear.

"Do you remember where Max was?" Maggie asked.

Grace shook her head. "No, but when I came down this afternoon to speak with the chef he and the chef were having a major screaming match."

"About what?"

"I have no idea."

It didn't matter. Whatever it was meant motive for Max. Maggie glanced over at the ski instructor.

"What are you two talking about?" Thompson asked gruffly, heaving his bulk into a chair by the table and groaning.

"Are you feeling all right, Mr. Thompson?" Grace asked.

"Doctor Toureille?" Maggie called to Manon. "We need you."

Manon rolled her eyes and didn't move.

"Manon, please," Serge said to her in frustration. "Help the man."

"Because *you* tell me to?" Manon snarled, but she was moving over to Thompson whose face was red and his breathing labored.

"It is because we are running out of air," Max said as he waved his arms to indicate the atmosphere in the room.

"Is that true?" Lisa asked, her cheeks pink. She began to fan herself although she was shivering in the cold. "Are we in danger of losing oxygen?"

"You should be worried about the danger of being stabbed by the killer among us!" Patel said, beginning to pace now.

Manon took Thompson's pulse and frowned. She took his temperature with the thermometer from the first aid kit and then picked up a napkin and wiped her hands.

"My money's on the *wog* for killing him," Thompson said, slurring his words. "I'm sure of it. Plain as day."

Maggie looked at Thompson's face and then tried to read

Manon's diagnosis from hers, but her expression was closed and guarded.

"It is a crime in our country to accuse without evidence!" Patel said hotly.

"His temperature is normal," Manon said, shaking the thermometer. "He has perhaps eaten a bad egg." She shrugged and packed up the first aid kit.

"I'm fine," Thompson said gruffly as he stood up. He pointed a finger at Raj Patel. "You were in the kitchen just before the avalanche."

"That is ridiculous!" Raj looked around at everyone's faces and then pointed at Max. "*He* hated the man! And it was *him* in the kitchen just before the avalanche!"

"*Incroyable!*" Max sputtered. "*Ce n'est pas ma faute!*"

"This isn't helping," Maggie said. "Everyone, please. Right now we need to worry about surviving until the rescuers can find us." She looked at Alys. "Let's conserve our batteries. Only one or two flashlights on at a time."

"I would say that is the opposite of what we should do!" Manon said. "We need all the light we can have! What if the killer isn't finished?"

An eruption of horror jumped up from the small group and poor Aishwarya actually whimpered. Maggie saw her reach for her husband's hand but he batted it away as if it were an annoyance.

"I agree with the doctor," Thompson said. "We need to keep all the lights on and stay together. But Mrs. Derne-yer is correct about staying quiet so that we may hear the search and rescue team."

Everyone nodded and took their places as if for a long vigil. Max and Alys sat on the floor in each other's arms and the newlywed Patels sat rigidly on chairs facing the now barricaded entrance to the lobby.

Grace still sat in the same chair she'd been in since dinner time. Serge and Lisa huddled together with Manon nearby and watchful. Lisa's head was bent and her shoulders were shaking.

How could this have happened? Maggie thought in bewilderment. When would they be rescued? Were people trying to dig them out even now?

A sob caught her attention and she looked at Lisa who was shaking her head vehemently. Maggie edged over to the couple.

"Everything okay?" she asked.

"What do you think?" Lisa said, tears streaking down her cheeks. "Of *course* it's not okay!"

Maggie glanced at Serge who looked helplessly back.

Lisa had a point though, Maggie thought as she wracked her brain to find something encouraging to say to her.

One thing was sure, none of them was okay.

20

A BAD END

Grace shifted in her chair as she watched Maggie kneel next to Lisa Mathers' chair and talk calmly with Lisa and Serge.

Had Maggie always been this assertive?

She watched the Indian couple sitting apart from the crowd and each other too. It was unbelievable to her that they were really newlyweds. Was it an arranged marriage? she wondered. She hated to fall into a stereotype but it certainly didn't look like a love match.

Like Windsor and I were?

Something deep inside of Grace flinched at the thought of her first husband. Yes, it had been a love match. Mostly.

It was only the terrible messy undoing of the love match that hadn't been so lovely.

Grace shivered at the sound of the creaking ceiling and realized that the sound and the resultant feeling matched perfectly how she had been living the last few years—under the shadow of imminent disaster.

She glanced at Maggie who was talking earnestly to the little concierge and Max now. It was unbelievable to Grace how

Maggie could have become this take-charge person when for so many years Grace would have described her, if not diffident then definitely unsure of herself.

That was the not the person Maggie had evolved into over the past few years.

Was that Laurent's influence? Grace thought of Laurent and felt a pang of guilt. She'd once been good friends with him too. But if Maggie was finding it difficult to forgive and forget, Laurent was not even trying. Not that Grace blamed him. She'd let everyone down terribly.

She thought back to the year in Paris when she'd chased after a younger man, pushing her children off on anyone who would mind them while she spent her time with him. And when he turned out to be someone who wanted only to take advantage of her and what little money she had—*well, let's just say I was the only one who hadn't seen it coming.*

And all of that would have been chalked up in the column of *Grace Finding Her Way* if it hadn't been for what had happened two years ago at Domaine St-Buvard.

Grace steeled herself to remember it. She'd gone through it enough times in therapy, she should be inured to it by now.

But it always astounded and wounded her anew when she remembered it.

She forced herself to remember how she'd lied to both Maggie and Laurent in order to get her catalog photographer to photograph little Mila—the only one of the children he was interested in. And then how her belated desperation to placate Taylor—after too many months and years of ignoring her—had created the ultimate lapse in judgment—one that led directly to Mila's kidnapping. That was on Grace. She may not have taken the child, but she was the one who'd allowed it to happen.

If it were me, I'd never forgive me either, she thought as she watched Maggie talking with Lisa and Serge.

And yet, here I am, begging for forgiveness with nothing to offer in return but contrition and even that difficult to believe by anybody who truly knows me.

Grace felt a thickness in her throat. She had a strong urge to push the thoughts away.

Was this her punishment? Did she even believe in such things? That her crime had been so terrible that being trapped under several tons of snow and ice with a roof about to collapse at any moment was appropriate come-uppance?

If that's so, then why is poor Maggie here? The only crime she ever committed was to trust and love me.

Maggie came back to the table, rubbing her arms against the cold. She cocked her head as she sat down to listen to the detective exchange a few words with the Patels. At least this time it appeared to be civil. In fact, young Mr. Patel seemed to be pointing out the direction of the ladies restroom to Thompson.

"I think if we can just stay warm and all in one spot, we'll be okay," Maggie said as she sat down next to Grace. She watched the detective disappear from the dining room in the direction of the restroom.

"He doesn't look good," Grace said.

"I know," Maggie said.

"Can you imagine the bad karma you'd have to have to get food poisoning during an avalanche?" Grace said.

Maggie laughed and Grace was grateful for the sound of it from her, even if it was gallows humor.

"Do you think we're safe here?" Grace asked.

Maggie squinted at the ceiling. "I have no idea."

"Is there another place to go that's safer?"

"The kitchen looks like it's about to crumble any moment. The bathroom might be okay but Mrs. Patel said it's just one room so we wouldn't all fit and the hallway definitely doesn't look safe."

"It's just that..." Grace hesitated and looked at the black wall of plate glass window. "If that window goes..."

"I know. Try not to think of it. It's just that all our other options are worse."

"I'm sorry, Maggie."

"Last time I checked you didn't cause the avalanche."

"You know what I'm saying."

"I know."

They sat quietly for a moment, hearing the window and the rafters creaking with the terrible weight on them. Regardless of Maggie's reassuring words, Grace fully expected the ceiling to come crashing down on top of them any minute now.

"Did you happen to see any wine when you were in the kitchen?" Grace asked.

Maggie laughed weakly. "Not a bad idea."

"I can't believe how in control you are through all this. You've changed."

"That's what motherhood does to you. I never really knew what was worth worrying about until I had kids."

"Well said."

It surprised Grace to see Manon and Serge standing so close together. Very probably it was because Manon had alienated every single other person in the place. But it was odd since his mistress Lisa also seemed to be a part of that group.

"Did you learn anything about who we're here with?" Grace asked.

"The newlyweds are Raj and Aishwarya Patel from London. He's a banker of some kind and she's a homemaker. Manon's a doctor as you know and her husband Serge is a high school teacher. They live in Paris."

"What about Lisa?"

"She's an author. Lisa Mathers. Ever hear of her?"

Grace shook her head.

"She writes thrillers. She met Serge when she was in Paris on a book tour."

"She'll have plenty to write about after this trip," Grace said.

"She looks ill. Is it only her foot that's injured?"

"I don't know. I agree, she looks sick."

"Speaking of which...Detective Thompson has been gone a long time. Should we be worried?"

A loud cracking noise rippled through the room and Grace grabbed Maggie's hand. They sat for a while in silence, holding hands and looking up at the ceiling. Grace could tell Maggie was holding her breath.

"When do you think they'll find us?" Grace whispered.

"I don't know how badly damaged the rest of the resort is," Maggie said. "If we assume the dining room took the brunt of the avalanche since it was facing the mountain, we can hope that everybody else in the place got out okay."

"What about the upstairs rooms?"

Maggie shivered. "Don't think about that," she said. "Let's just hope nobody who had a mountain view was in their rooms at the time."

Both of our rooms face the mountain, Grace realized. As bad as things were down here, it was better than if they'd been in their rooms when the avalanche hit.

"Pretty wild about the chef," Grace said.

"I keep trying to figure out who was near him tonight."

"Mr. Patel seems to think Max had the greatest opportunity."

"He had the most access," Maggie admitted. "And from what you said, motive too."

Maggie turned to stare at Max where he sat talking with Alys.

"Why were you in the kitchen before dinner?" Maggie asked without taking her eyes off Max.

"Making sure we didn't get poisoned tonight."

Maggie laughed and Grace took comfort from that.

Now if I can just keep us in crisis mode for our entire friendship, we'll get along fine.

"I'm sorry about what I said earlier," Maggie said.

"Don't be. You were right."

"Still shouldn't have said it."

"If we have any hope at all of being friends again one day, you should have."

∼

Maggie could see Aishwarya looking at her from three tables away, The new bride's eyes were beseeching but her face was a mask of determination.

"Her husband's making her come over here," Grace whispered. "What an ass."

Maggie agreed. He was making her do something against her will. Maggie saw it in her hesitation and resistance as Aishwarya tightened her grip on the tablecloth around her and focused her gaze on Maggie.

Raj Patel leaned back in his chair and crossed his arms.

"He's made a fool of himself," Grace said under her breath, "and now he wants something."

"Hello, Mrs. Patel," Maggie said and gestured to the chair next to her. It was frankly unbelievable that they were still acting like life was normal at the moment but given that there was nowhere else to go and nothing else to do, a little courtesy probably wasn't the worst way in the world to handle things.

"I am so sorry to bother you," Aishwarya said. She stopped short of actually joining Maggie and Grace at their table. "We have no water."

Grace pushed the pitcher of water across the table toward her. "Help yourself."

"Are you all right, Mrs. Patel?" Maggie asked as she glanced over the woman's shoulder at her husband who was glaring at them.

"Please call me Aishwarya. I am fine but my husband is interested in knowing if someone will be procuring food for us."

"Unbelievable," Grace said.

Maggie wanted to shush Grace but Aishwarya had already heard her. In any case surely she had many times had to endure the world's harsh assessment of her husband.

"The kitchen is unsafe," Maggie said. "But I believe we'll be rescued before we need to worry about food."

"Of course," Aishwarya said picking up the water pitcher with both hands.

"You are more than welcome to join us at our table, Aishwarya," Grace said.

Maggie noted that Grace hadn't extended the invitation to Aishwarya's husband.

"Is it safer over here, do you think?" Aishwarya asked.

"Nobody knows," Maggie said. "But you're welcome to sit with us if you'd like. Your husband too, of course."

"Thank you," Aishwarya said and she smiled tiredly. "But we are fine." She gave a slight nod and turned with the water pitcher to hurry back to her husband.

"I can't believe they're on their honeymoon," Grace murmured as she watched Aishwarya retreat.

"I know."

Another loud crack came from the giant wall of black snow pressed up against the picture window. Both Maggie and Grace jumped at the sound. Maggie moved her chair to sit closer to Grace. She wasn't sure why, she just needed to be near her right now.

"What do you think, darling?" Grace said in a low voice. "Are we going to get out of this alive?"

Maggie felt a cold finger of fear draw down her spine. She shivered against the sensation. *No.* They *had* to get out of this. She and Grace both had children. Maggie had Laurent. This was a terrible situation to be sure but it *wasn't* going to end in tragedy.

That was just not acceptable.

Max sat on the floor with his arm around Alys, which surprised Maggie. She'd already seen that the concierge was nervous and tearful—not at all good under pressure. It did seem that the way Max was relating to Alys was closer to how a father might than a lover but they were both French and Maggie had long since stopped trying to decipher the affairs of the heart in France.

In any case, if they were lovers, what did that mean as far as Max being a likely suspect for killing LeFleur? Anything?

Serge, Manon and Lisa still sat together like old friends except when Maggie picked up pieces of dialogue from them it was alternately spiteful and defensive. She was at a loss to understand why the three would choose to sit together.

"I need to check on Thompson," she said to Grace.

"I'll go with you."

"No. I'll make the doctor go with me. You stay here and keep your eye on Max."

"You think he killed the chef?"

"He seems more likely than anyone else."

"Do you think he's finished or should we be worried?" Grace said, narrowing her eyes at Max as he held Alys and spoke to her in a low voice.

"I have no idea."

Maggie stood and went over to Manon who was speaking in forceful French invective to her husband.

"Excuse me," Maggie said. "Madame Toureille? *Docteur*? I need you to come with me to check on Mr. Thompson."

Maggie was ready for Manon to resist but the woman obviously knew it would be an argument she wouldn't win. She sighed dramatically and gave her husband a warning look although for the life of her Maggie couldn't imagine what he and Lisa could get up to in a public dining room in Manon's absence.

Manon was wiry and lithe and she walked lightly, something Maggie was grateful for. She didn't know what effect loud noises or a heavy tread might have on the precarious positioning of the overhead beams but she'd rather not find out.

She moved behind the doctor as they skirted the Patels' table and then walked down the short hall off the dining room. Now for the first time, Maggie saw that a portion of the ceiling had in fact already come down in the hall, making access to the men's room impossible. They stepped over a beam that lay across the carpeted hall.

The top part of the fish tank had been shattered in the avalanche and much of the water had seeped out onto the carpet which was sodden where they walked. The bodies of the many colorful fish were scattered on the rug or floating in the blue water that was left in the aquarium.

Maggie was glad Manon didn't want to speak. It took all Maggie's concentration to hold the flashlight such that the beam showed them where to put their feet. Once they were at the door to the ladies room, Manon didn't hesitate but pushed on it with both hands.

It wouldn't budge.

Maggie moved past Manon and put her shoulder into it. Something was obstructing the door's opening. She wondered if more of the ceiling had possibly come down since the first avalanche. They hadn't heard any loud noise from the dining room and Maggie turned to see what she could detect from where she stood. She couldn't hear voices or sounds from the dining room.

"Detective Thompson?" Maggie called through the crack in the door.

There was no answer.

"Are you sure he went to *this* bathroom?" Manon asked with annoyance.

Maggie pushed harder on the door and felt it give. She directed the light from her flashlight through the crack.

She could see why the door wouldn't open.

It was blocked by Thompson's body.

21

NIGHT OF THE SOUL

With both Maggie and Manon putting their shoulders to the bathroom door, they managed to push it open. Maggie glanced around the small room which had only a toilet and sink. The detective's body was wedged behind the half-open door.

He was very still and Maggie felt her heart drop. He was *too* still.

With her heartbeat racing, she focused her flashlight beam on him while Manon squeezed through the opening and knelt to examine him. There were no obvious wounds that Maggie could see but there was white foam around the corners of his mouth.

"Is he breathing?" Maggie asked.

"*Non.* He is dead."

Maggie felt a sudden weakness in her knees.

"Does it look like a...a heart attack or something?" Maggie asked.

What did this mean? Did someone kill him too?

Manon gave her a withering look. "How I am telling something like that without any diagnostic tools?"

"What is that white stuff around his lips?"

Manon turned back to the body and then leaned over and sniffed at his mouth. She straightened.

"It could be poison," she said. "But only an autopsy will tell us for sure."

"I need you to help me drag him out of here."

"*Mais non!* Why?"

"Because we need this room," Maggie said impatiently. "Unless you're okay with stepping over a dead body every time you need to—"

"Okay, okay," Manon said.

Maggie was tempted to make Max come help but she felt strongly they all needed to move around as little as possible. She and Manon were already here. They'd do what needed to be done.

Minutes later, after maneuvering the detective's body to the small debris-strewn alcove leading to the barricaded men's room door, they rejoined the others.

Max and Alys were on their feet as if waiting for them. Serge walked across the dining room to meet them.

"What did you find?" Serge asked his wife. "Where is the detective?"

"Look, everyone," Maggie said, raising her voice to get everyone's attention. "I think we need to stay in one spot. I don't know how unstable the ceiling is but moving around won't help things."

"What happened to the detective?" Lisa called out, her voice bordering on the hysterical.

Maggie knew she had to tell them, but she also knew the knowledge was not going to make things easier.

Not by a long shot.

"He has been murdered!" Manon said to Lisa. "Just as in the cheap novels you write."

Alys shrieked and clapped a hand to her mouth. Maggie caught the sight of Aishwarya lurching to her feet, her eyes bulging with horror.

"Please everyone, stay calm," Maggie said, narrowing her eyes indictingly at Manon. "We don't know he was murdered."

"How?" Raj Patel hurried over to them, knocking over two chairs in the process and leaving his now nearly hysterical wife back at their table. "*How* is he dead? I demand to know!"

"Look," Maggie said, feeling a headache coming on. "He might very well have had a heart attack over the strain of all this. He was older and overweight. Isn't that right, Dr. Toureille?"

Manon shrugged. "It is my professional opinion that he was poisoned," she said. "I smelled almonds on his breath."

"Is that true?" Alys said in a shrill voice, her eyes damp and overly bright. "Someone *poisoned* Monsieur Thompson?"

"That is *not* necessarily true!" Maggie said in frustration. "We can't jump to conclusions like this!"

"But he *is* dead," Grace said softly.

Maggie turned to look at her. Grace was staring at the chair that Thompson had sat in at dinner. Maggie knew what she was thinking. One minute he was here, and the next...

"Monsieur Fountainbleu?" Maggie said turning to Max. "Is there wine by any chance? I think that would be a good idea about now."

He nodded, glanced at Alys and then turned to walk toward the kitchen.

"Carefully, please, Max," Maggie urged, not at all sure that wine was a good idea but knowing she needed to distract everyone from the second dead body found in less than an hour.

The wine helped.

While the Patels continued to stay to themselves, Max and Alys moved closer to Maggie and Grace's table. Maggie wasn't sure why she felt relieved about that. Maybe because she didn't want to think Max was the killer and for some reason opting to sit with her and Grace didn't feel like something a psychopathic serial killer would do.

Is that what this was? A serial killing? Was Thompson's death accidental? Natural causes?

Manon seemed convinced he had been poisoned and while her credibility wasn't the best as far as Maggie was concerned, if it *was* a poisoning it would help explain things. If vomiting up foam wasn't one of the symptoms of an overweight guy keeling over from a heart attack but was in fact a symptom of a fatal poisoning, then the question had to be: *Was Thompson the intended target?*

And if he was, was it random? Because if *that* was true, then Maggie could stop looking for motive or reasons right now.

She sighed heavily.

When were the rescuers coming? Did they even know the avalanche had hit the resort? Had the other people in the resort gotten out and raised the alarm?

Or were they all dead?

She glanced at her cellphone and saw the battery was about to give out. It was nearly ten o'clock. It had been two hours since the avalanche had hit.

It felt like much longer.

Laurent must be wondering why she hadn't called. Unless he figured she and Grace had lost track of time.

A sudden chill invaded her as she realized that Laurent wouldn't be wondering what happened at all. He'd have heard about the avalanche on the news.

He must be out of his mind with worry.

Shaking off the thought—one that she could presently do nothing about—she topped up her glass of Bordeaux. Max had found a half dozen bottles and also brought a basket of packaged cheese biscuits. Nobody needed to be told that any of the open food in the kitchen might be tainted.

Besides, with LeFleur's body still lying in his own gore, nobody wanted to go into the kitchen.

"Penny for them?" Grace said as she opened a packet of the savory cheese biscuits and offered one to Maggie.

"I was thinking about Thompson," Maggie said, declining the cracker. "If he was poisoned, was it an accident?"

"You mean he might have sampled something intended for someone else when he went into the kitchen?"

"He'd already been served when I came into the dining room," Maggie said. "He picked up his whole plate when he joined us."

"So he was poisoned that soon?"

"I don't know. A part of me thinks he ate something not intended for him. But I don't know why I think that."

They sat in silence for a moment. Maggie could hear the pings and snaps of the ice as it cracked above them. Or was it the beams? She tried to shake off the image of the whole ceiling crashing down on top of them.

It either would or it wouldn't. There was nothing she could do about it either way.

"Taylor's pregnant," Grace said.

Maggie's mouth fell open and she turned to Grace. "Oh, Grace, no."

"I don't know why I'm surprised." Grace wiped a tear from her cheek. "She probably did it just to upset me. You know how she is."

"Who's the boy?"

"She won't say."

"Does she want to keep it?"

Grace took a long swig of her wine. "I don't know," she said. "I'm trying not to come down too heavy on her. If I underscore how much I need her to have the baby and give it up, she'll abort it."

"What does Windsor say?"

Grace shook her head. "He's still in the stage where this is all my fault."

"I'm so sorry, Grace." Maggie thought of little Mila and how upset *she* would be if this happened to her. Taylor was fifteen. She'd always been difficult but up to now she'd only made herself and her parents miserable.

"What are you going to do?"

"She's with Windsor and Susie at the moment," Grace said. "I think they're all pretending this is normal or a right of passage or something. Susie was talking about a baby shower."

"What does Zouzou think of all this?"

Grace shook her head. "I'm sure it hasn't escaped your notice that Zouzou has developed her own set of problems."

"Any idea why?" Maggie knew teenagers could be difficult but Zouzou was barely a preteen.

"I'm guessing it's bad mothering," Grace said.

"Oh, Grace." Maggie didn't know what else to say. She tried to remember a time back a few thousand years ago when she'd envied Grace. Envied her house, her wealth, her comfort and insouiance with the world, her rare ability to make laughter sound like silver bells on the wind.

"Did I pick up that your mother is worried about your dad?" Grace said, changing the subject. "What's going on with him?"

"He has Alzheimer's."

"Darling, I'm so sorry. "

"Thanks. She wants me to come back to the States and help her with him."

"Has she looked to see the kind of help that's available back in Atlanta?"

"I think she figures that's what I'm here for."

"Oh, darling, you have a very busy life and a family of your own. Would it even be possible? Laurent leaving the vineyard and relocating to Atlanta?"

"I don't think so. I guess we'd be looking at a transatlantic relationship. Me and the kids in Atlanta, him in France."

"Oh, sweetie. I'm so sorry."

"Yeah. We'll sort it out somehow I guess."

They drank in silence for a moment with only the urgent unintelligible whisperings from Raj and Aishwarya Patel.

"How's Danielle?" Graced asked.

"Her cancer is in remission," Maggie said. "Just in time for Jean-Luc to start to weaken."

"Oh, no! I was sure Jean-Luc would outlive us all."

"Me, too. He's the closest thing to a father that Laurent has—although Laurent would never admit it."

Grace laughed. "Do you remember the first time we got together with Connor and Jean-Luc was there? That was when you weren't too sure about Jean-Luc."

"I think I was more unsure of Connor," Maggie said wryly. She reached out and squeezed Grace's hand. Connor was Zouzou's biological father although he died before he could find that out. It was Windsor's discovery of that fact that had hastened the dissolution of his marriage to Grace.

"Connor was an original," Grace said, her eyes glistening with tears.

"He definitely was that."

"Laurent didn't like him, did he?"

"Not much," Maggie admitted. "But you know Laurent. He still looks at the world through the eyes of a con artist half the time. And he saw Connor as one of his own breed."

"You'd think that would make him like him all the more."

"I don't think Laurent sees any honor or romantic charm in what he used to do."

"Ah well." Another long pause. "I can't believe you still have the dog that Madame Renoir gave you so many years ago. Little Petit-Four."

"She's old now," Maggie said. "It will break my heart when I lose her. What happened to yours?"

"We gave her to one of Taylor's nannies when we moved back to the States."

In the beat of silence between them, Maggie heard the ceiling moan as if it were breathing.

"I think Laurent is frustrated with the vineyard," she said.

"Really? Based on what?"

Maggie shrugged. "He's had to compromise with it so many times. From selling our wine to the co-op to the boutique and now to the limited partnership. I think he feels it's less a family farm somehow. And worse, Jemmy isn't at all interested in following in his father's footsteps."

"Well, Jemmy's only seven. There's still plenty of time for him to drink Laurent's Kool-Aid."

"I don't know. Jemmy has a more scholarly bent than Laurent. Somehow I can't see him picking grapes and waiting for the weather to determine if the year was a good one or not."

"I wouldn't count him out yet."

"Tell me about the new man in your life," Maggie said. She knew she should have asked before now. She knew Grace took it as a sign of the schism between them that she hadn't. And Grace would have been right.

"He's older."

"I heard that," Maggie said. When Grace raised an eyebrow, Maggie said, "You know Laurent speaks to Windsor from time to time."

"Ah. Well, his name is Garner. He's wealthy and he's retired. He used to teach economics at Emory."

"So he's smart."

"He is. He's also careful. Widowed with two grown children. They don't like me."

"Why not?"

"Mostly because I'm dating their dad. I haven't met them yet."

"Then how do you know they don't like you?"

"A few months back just before Garner's birthday I wrote a note to Rachel, his daughter—she lives in Atlanta—inviting her to a small dinner I was having for him. She declined in no uncertain terms."

"Did you tell Garner?"

"Didn't seem any point. I'm trying to do things differently this time around, Maggie. Trying to be less selfish. Trying to deserve the blessings I'm given."

"Sounds like a plan."

"I was a fool to divorce Windsor."

"Do you still love him?"

"No, not at all. But I let the marriage go too easily. And the divorce affected us all much worse than I'd imagined. Not just the girls but me too. Windsor, as you know, bounced back pretty well."

"I'd like to meet Garner someday," Maggie said.

"I know you'll like him. I even think Laurent will like him."

"It's enough that *you* do."

"That's sweet, darling. But it's not true. It's never enough. That's one thing I've learned through all this. If I've learned anything."

After they finished their wine, Maggie saw that everyone else in the group had settled down to sleep. It was somewhat amazing to her that they could still hear no noise at all from any search and rescue attempts.

But getting rest if at all possible was a good idea. Maggie didn't know what the next day would bring but likely they would need all their energy for whatever it was. Gathering a few more tablecloths, she and Grace curled up on the floor, careful not to lean against any load-bearing walls. With a quick hand-squeeze to say goodnight and mark the night of sharing, Maggie closed her eyes and fell fast asleep.

Later in the middle of the night, she found herself wrestling with a dream that she knew to be a dream but that still forced her to fight for breath. She was struggling to sit up and felt a heavy weight on her chest. It moved to her mouth and nose and she realized it was snow. She was suffocating beneath the bombardment of the freezing snow of the avalanche that had finally found its way into the dining room.

Gasping for air, her terror ratcheted up into her throat, Maggie finally broke free of the dream and sat bolt upright. Her skin was vibrating in fear and premonition.

Steadying herself by placing both hands on the cold carpet beside her, she took in a long breath and waited for her eyes to adjust to the darkness. She looked around to see all the tablecloth covered mounds of the people sleeping around her. All except one.

Grace was gone.

22

THAT GOOD NIGHT

The sight of a tall church spire on the horizon heralded Laurent's approach to the twelfth-century Cistercian monastery in the village of Pont l'Abbe. The monastery Abbaye de Sainte-Trinité lay just on the village outskirts.

Laurent tried to remember what he knew of the monastery. He remembered hearing that it was an active order maintained by a dozen or so Benedictine monks but what their ministry was he didn't know. He seemed to vaguely recall that the monastery had capabilities for making wine—or perhaps storing it—but there was no longer any adjoining land to plant vines.

As he drove through the village, he felt his heartbeat speed up. What if Zouzou wasn't there? How would she possibly have gotten this far from Domaine St-Buvard? The monastery was situated on the far side of the village, bordered to the north by Eduard Marceau's vineyard.

Once through Ponte l'Abbe, Laurent caught glimpses of the buildings ahead that comprised the monastery. A small stone chapel—with its roof long blown out—sat next to an ancient rectory and an even older arrangement of low-roofed buildings—once used as stables. Beyond that were the monastery's gardens.

The winding drive from the village to the front door of the main building—a sprawling stone structure visible for miles—was pocked with rocks and encroaching weeds. A broken stone curtain wall enclosed the monastery on two sides. As Laurent parked on the gravel lot in front, he noted the cylindrical turrets and towers—looking very like a medieval castle—and he wondered at the monastery's history. From his school days he knew that most monasteries in France had been destroyed or decommissioned after the French Revolution but not much about what happened to them after that.

A mammoth set of wooden doors with iron hinges loomed ten feet over Laurent's head at the center of the main building. It didn't take much imagination to believe that inside those doors was a microcosm of peace and serenity untouched by the outside world.

Before Laurent had a chance to pound on the massive door, a smaller door built into one of the double doors swung open to reveal a monk in dark robes.

The monk was short but powerfully built with a barrel chest and a head of wavy white hair. His eyes were small and beady but his smile was real, showing a row of white teeth.

"We have been expecting you, Monsieur," the monk said as he stepped out of the way so that Laurent could enter. "Zouzou told us you would come."

A shudder of relief swept through Laurent at the man's words, but was followed closely by a spasm of fury. His reaction must have been visible to the monk as he ushered Laurent through the door.

"Oh, dear," the monk said. "She said you knew she was here. Am I to understand that is not true?"

The stone foyer where Laurent now stood reverberated with the sounds of people and children. Down the nearest hall he caught glimpses of people moving about. He could smell food cooking.

"What is it that you are doing here?" Laurent said, ignoring the monk's question and moving down the hall in the direction of the activity. He hadn't walked all the way down the hall before he answered his own question.

The hall opened up into a main area featuring a high arched ceiling of rock over slate floors and stone walls that showcased tall narrow windows that let in the warmth from several shafts of the weak winter sun. Children ran laughing across the stone floor throwing balls. There were even dogs, barking and running along with the children.

Laurent saw several groups of men and women huddled at tables with bowls of steaming soup in their hands. They watched him warily. Not gypsies. He could see that immediately. Possibly refugees. Some foreign. Some French. But all poor. And desperate.

Behind them was a line of monks ladling up soup into bowls and handing out bread. Laurent could hear the wind whistling through the cracks in the stone walls. The scene was warm but the temperature in the cavernous room was still unpleasantly cold.

"You are housing these people?" Laurent asked, turning to the monk.

"Yes. I am Frère Jean by the way. I am sorry about Zouzou. There are many people here as you see and the children can be very difficult to keep track of."

"There have been reports of thefts around St-Buvard," Laurent said as he scanned the crowd of people for the one he sought.

"I am sorry to hear that. Please come in, Monsieur. I will send for Zouzou."

Laurent moved toward the central fireplace that anchored the large room. A stack of firewood was piled beside it and a boy about Zouzou's age stood and diligently fed the fire. He glanced at Laurent.

Beeswax candles sat on every table but flickered with the drafts that continually blew through the room.

"They are homeless?" Laurent asked the monk as he stretched his hands out to the fire. He knew he should call Elspeth to let her know about Zouzou but he'd left the phone in the car. A few minutes more wouldn't hurt.

"They have found their way to us mostly through word of mouth. The east has shown a severe downturn in jobs. Some are simply escaping unlivable situations. We do not ask. Once they come—on their way to Nîmes or the coast—they often stay longer than anticipated."

"Because there are no jobs for them in Nîmes or the coast?"

"These are people willing to work, Monsieur. We have plumbers, day laborers, even a dental hygienist. One man ran a *boulangerie* but the cost of butter soon made it impossible for his employers to keep him on. He is here with his family. These are proud people. They are not looking for charity. They are looking for a community that wants them."

"And that is you?"

"Our order here at Abbaye de Sainte-Trinité has made a promise of stability," Frère Jean said.

Laurent frowned and raised an eyebrow.

"It means we have sworn to remain in the same community in order to serve that community."

Laurent took in the sight of the homeless families and the playing children.

"Unlike some orders that focus solely on contemplation," Frère Jean continued, "our emphasis is an active ministry. As you see."

"It looks as if you are at your limit. Or beyond."

"Yes, it is bedlam at the moment," Frère Jean said. "But trust me when I say Abbaye de Sainte-Trinité is a place of scheduled silence and spirituality, liturgical prayer and community life. Every one of these people helps us fulfill our ministry."

"Are you able to adequately feed and house them?" Laurent asked.

"It is difficult," the monk admitted looking around the room. There were at least fifty people around the tables. "If it were spring, they could help us work the monastery gardens. But alas, it is winter and so we struggle."

"How are you supporting them?"

"We take alms from the village church."

"And what do the villagers think of this?"

For the first time, Laurent saw a pinched expression on the monk's face, his lips pressed into a white line.

"The villagers go to their warm beds each night with full stomachs," he said. "They do not worry about where their children are or when they will be fed next."

"But perhaps they do worry about people breaking into their homes and garages."

The monk sighed. "Some of the young ones go out at night. We can't stop them."

"You can forbid the families to remain as long as their children do not follow your rules."

Frère Jean looked at Laurent and smiled sadly. "No, Monsieur. We cannot."

As the monk spoke, Laurent saw Zouzou walking slowly and sullenly toward him from the back of the crowd and it occurred to him that that policy wasn't exactly working for him either.

On the drive back, Laurent didn't press Zouzou to explain herself. She held herself tightly in the passenger seat, her arms hugging her chest and Laurent put the heat up higher although he did not really think she was cold.

After he called both Elspeth and Danielle to tell them that Zouzou was safe, he turned off the road that would have taken them directly back to Domaine St-Buvard. If Zouzou knew the area well enough to know, she didn't comment on it and they drove in silence for another thirty minutes. In that time, Zouzou propped her chin on her hand to watch the bleak winter landscape as it flew by outside the car. At one point she even yawned and Laurent wondered where and how the child had slept last night.

"You didn't know I was gone, did you?" she said, not looking at him.

Encouraged by the fact that she was at least talking, Laurent took his time answering. He was sure she wouldn't appreciate him lying to her. He never much cared for that himself.

"*Non*," he said finally. "I thought all was well with my world."

She turned to look at him and for a moment he thought she would say more but in the end she just turned to look back out the window.

When they came to the next village, St-Lavau, Laurent drove down the main street and parked against a curb in front of a *patisserie*.

"Why are we here?" Zouzou asked.

Lauren shrugged. "It is lunch time," he said, getting out of the car.

Zouzou hesitated and then slowly released her seatbelt and got out too, following Laurent to the restaurant off the main square.

He wasn't sure why he hadn't thought of doing this before. He knew that Maggie often accused him of being too simplistic but just as the English like their cup of tea to soothe jangled nerves or buffer against bad news, in Laurent's world there were very few things that weren't improved upon by the enjoyment of good, nourishing food.

He entered the restaurant, aware that Zouzou was behind him. Tin ceiling tiles stamped with ornate patterns and hardwood floors polished to a gleam gave the inside of the little bistro an immediate cozy feel. Heavy toile café curtains hung against the large windows facing the street, and gilded antique frames and mirrors on the dark walls afforded a touch of understated elegance that merged with a feel of *en famille*.

A waiter greeted them and sat them in a booth near the fireplace positioned at the back of the room. It was late for lunch and there were only four or five other diners in the restaurant. Laurent ordered without looking at the menu.

"I'm not hungry," Zouzou said, her eyes big as she looked around the restaurant.

The waiter brought wine and poured Laurent's glass. Laurent turned over the small juice glass in front of Zouzou and dribbled a small amount of wine into it.

"A sip or two won't hurt," he said.

Zouzou's eyes grew wider and she looked at Laurent as if expecting a trick of some kind.

"Mom won't like it," she said, reaching for her glass.

They sat quietly in the restaurant until the waiter returned and set a large ceramic tureen of potato soup in the center of the table. He placed a silver soupspoon by each of their napkins. Another waiter set down a basket of fresh baked bread.

Laurent waited until the waiter left and then ladled soup into each of their bowls.

Zouzou picked up her spoon. "There's cream in this," she said.

"*Oui*. That's what makes it good."

"I'm not allowed to have cream. It has too many calories."

Laurent narrowed his eyes and handed her a piece of bread.

"I'm not allowed," Zouzou said shaking her head.

"You are not allowed to have bread?"

Zouzou's eyes filled with tears.

"Man cannot live without bread," Laurent said putting the chunk of bread next to her bowl. "Or little girls either."

"Mom says—"

"Your mother eats bread."

"My mother isn't fat."

"Neither are you."

Zouzou dropped her spoon in her bowl with a clank and put her hands in her lap, her head bowed.

Laurent sighed and took a long sip of his wine.

"What if I were to tell you," he said, "that you could be as slim as you like and still enjoy bread? *And* soup with cream?"

Zouzou looked up at him, her eyes luminous with unshed tears. "Really?"

"Do you want me to teach you how?"

She nodded, her lips parting slightly.

"*Bon*. Eat your soup."

Zouzou snatched up her spoon and took the first taste. "It's so good," she said. "Are you sure I'm allowed to eat this?"

"I am sure, *chérie*," Laurent said sadly, wondering what Grace or Windsor or someone had said to the child to make her afraid to eat a bowl of soup.

No wonder she sneaks candy alone in her bedroom.

Zouzou took a tentative sip of the wine and made a face.

"It does not taste like Coca, does it?" Laurent said, hiding a small smile.

"No."

They ate quietly for several minutes and when the waiter came back he brought two wedges of Quiche Lorraine and set the plates before them. Zouzou wolfed down several bites of the quiche before Laurent touched her hand holding her fork.

"The soup has taken the edge off your hunger," he said. "Now is when you look about and focus on your surroundings, your dinner companion." He grinned and she smiled tentatively back. "You may now appreciate the texture and flavors of your meal because you are no longer starving, eh?"

"I wish you were my father," she said suddenly. "Daddy loves Taylor more than me. And now he and Susie are going to adopt Taylor's baby and they'll love him more than me too."

Laurent had heard of Taylor's pregnancy of course but not that Windsor was thinking of raising the baby himself.

"Does it matter so much who loves whom more?" he asked.

"Yes."

Laurent shrugged. "Perhaps you will not be able to make him love you the most. Are you prepared for that?"

"No. I want him to."

"Then I am afraid you are going to be unhappy in your life."

"Do you think I should just give up?"

"Are you asking if you should give up trying to make people love you in a certain way? Yes. Of course."

They ate in silence and then Zouzou put her fork down. She looked at Laurent with surprise. "I'm full."

"Your appetite will return for dinner."

"The kids at school back in Atlanta are mean to me," Zouzou said. "They call me fat."

Laurent didn't ask her why she cared what the other kids thought. She was a child. Of course she cared.

"My mom named me *Zouzou* which sounds like I'm a Paris dancer or something. But I don't fit my name. The kids back home call me Choochoo. You know, like a train? Coz I'm big like one."

Laurent felt a flash of irritation at *the kids back home.*

"And your new friend Giselle?" he asked. "The one you met in the village?"

"She's nice. She thought I was awesome because I'm American. It was cool to be popular for a change, you know? She invited me over for a sleepover and I met her at the foot of the garden yesterday before it got dark." She looked up at Laurent and blushed. "I'm sorry for leaving without telling anyone."

You mean without asking anyone, Laurent thought, but he only nodded.

"Is it true you can really teach me to be thin and eat bread too?"

"If you do everything I tell you," he said mock sternly. "You have had trouble minding what I say since you've come to Domaine St-Buvard."

"I know. I'm sorry. I'll do everything you tell me from now on. I promise."

"*Bon*. We have a deal."

"But my mom and I are leaving France next week. How are you going to teach me from long distance?"

"Perhaps there is another way."

"You mean like maybe I can stay with you in France?" Zouzou said excitedly.

"We shall see," Laurent said, not at all sure what he meant by that.

23

TURN, TURN, TURN

The first place Maggie ran to was the ladies bathroom. Her cellphone battery was dead and she couldn't see in the dark to find a flashlight so she stumbled blindly through the darkened dining room, overturning empty food carts and knocking over chairs.

She reached the hall leading to the ladies room and saw it was a dark cavern. In frustration, she turned back and called out.

"I need a flashlight! Please, hurry!"

By now everyone was awake. A harsh beam of light struck Maggie full in the face and she squinted and reached out for it at the same time.

"What is it?" Raj Patel said. "Is it help? Have they found us?"

"I need the flashlight, Raj," Maggie said, lurching toward the light. "Please!"

She tripped over an upended chair and sprawled on the carpet in front of him. He frowned and played the beam toward the entrance to the hall where she had come.

"So it is not rescue?" he said.

Maggie jumped to her feet and snatched the flashlight from

him. Taken aback for a moment, he allowed her to get a few steps away.

"Hey! I need that!" he shouted as he lunged at her and grabbed the flashlight back.

"My friend is missing," Maggie said desperately, her mouth suddenly dry. "Please!"

"Who is missing?" Lisa called out. "Is it the other American?"

Alys and Max came to where Maggie stood with Raj. Alys handed Maggie her flashlight.

"Perhaps she is in the toilet?" Alys said as Maggie gratefully took the light and turned to run back to the hall.

Careful not to fall over the piles of debris in her path, Maggie made her way through the small hall.

"Grace?" she called. "Are you there?"

She ran down the hall, feeling the sodden carpet beneath her shoes from where the fish tank continued to leak. She reached the restroom door and pushed it open. The interior was immediately illuminated by her flashlight beam.

Empty.

Maggie shook her head in denial and bit her bottom lip in building panic.

Where could she be?

Turning, she forced herself not to run back down the hallway to the entrance of the dining room.

"Did you find her?" Alys called as Maggie came into the dining room. Maggie didn't waste time answering. She went toward the kitchen.

"Do not go in there, Madame!" Max called out. "It is unstable!"

Why doesn't he want me to go in there? Maggie thought with hysteria. *Is it because he knows Grace is in there? Dying? Already dead?*

She plunged into the kitchen, raking the interior with the beam of her light. A giant rack of copper pots and pans sat on the floor in the middle of the room where it had fallen. It was nearly hidden by two large oak beams that had fallen on top of it. Stainless steel appliances lined the far wall—a massive refrigerator whose door had popped open revealing its dark interior. A line of stainless steel sinks were now filled with plaster and broken pieces of wood. Three gas stoves were squashed flat under the weight of another of the ceiling beams.

Maggie moved gingerly past the pantry door. LeFleur's body was where she'd last seen it and while she hated to destroy the crime scene by stepping over it, she had no other choice. Careful not to touch any beams, columns or interior walls, Maggie made her way to the center of the kitchen. A wall of ovens had fallen into the middle, blocking her way to the row of sinks.

"Grace!" she called again and held her breath to listen for the reply. She heard only the sound of her own panicked breathing, the hysterical beating of her own heart.

"Madame?" Max spoke from where he stood by the swinging doors.

"Don't come in here," Maggie said. Her worry about Max dislodging wreckage was not as great as her growing belief that he was here only to see if Maggie would find what he had done to Grace.

Why would Max hurt Grace? Why would anyone? Because if there was no motive and this was all random, then the killer could be anyone.

Maggie spent the next ten minutes walking carefully to every cabinet and cupboard in the kitchen she could reach, her stomach roiling in fear as she shined her light on them all.

Nothing.

Grace wasn't in the kitchen.

Maggie made her way across the kitchen, her heart heavy with disappointment and fear.

Where is she? Why did she leave in the middle of the night? What could possibly have beckoned her?

But Maggie knew what. She knew only too well. And she also knew that if she was right then Grace's disappearance was her fault. And that was because Grace would have done all manner of stupid stunts to show Maggie they could operate as a team again.

Like the old days.

Maggie hesitated, trying to listen to any possible sounds that might tell her where Grace was or that *somebody* on the outside was working to free them.

The only sound she heard was a shout from the dining room. Her heart pounding, Maggie bolted toward the direction of the shouting.

They were all grouped around the table where Maggie had last seen Grace. Her heart sped up in anticipation. Had she not searched the area well enough? Was it possible that Grace was there all along?

"What is it?" Maggie asked. "Did you find her?"

Alys turned to Maggie, her face stricken with fear and dread.

"It is Madame Toureille," she said. "We cannot find her."

24

CHECKMATE

At over six foot five, Laurent easily gave the appearance of filling the farmhouse kitchen as he moved from stove to oven, picking up utensils from the counter and arranging crockery and glassware as he moved.

Zouzou stood next to Laurent at the stove as he put a chunk of butter into a hot skillet on the stove.

"The eggs are beaten, yes?" Laurent asked. "But not too much."

"I think so," Zouzou said as she looked into the bowl of eggs she held in her hands.

"*Bon,*" he said. "Put them in now."

Zouzou carefully slid the beaten eggs into the hot pan and reached for a wooden spoon.

"Not yet," Laurent said. "Let the curds set first."

"It smells really good," Zouzou said, not taking her eyes off the pan.

"Now you may stir to keep it from sticking on the bottom," Laurent said, turning away to allow Zouzou to handle the task on her own.

He sliced several pieces of *pain de mie* and put them in the toaster.

"Hey! I want to help!" Jemmy said as he and Mila ran into the room and took their seats at the kitchen counter. Maggie's little dog Petit-Four looked up from where she was curled up on the couch and tracked the children as they moved into the kitchen.

"*Non*," Laurent said setting glasses of juice down in front of both of them. "Zouzou has it handled." He briefly cupped his hand on Mila's cheek and his daughter smiled at him. He felt his heart expand in his chest at her smile. She was always in a good mood, always ready to smile and see the best in the world.

He wondered how long that would last.

"I think they're done, Oncle Laurent," Zouzou said in a nervous voice.

Laurent turned to the stove and snapped the fire off under the pan.

"They will cook a little longer in the pan. Get the plates and napkins."

While Zouzou turned to do the much less demanding task of setting places Laurent didn't fool himself into thinking he had solved her problems with one talk and a scrambled egg lesson. There was much that worried Zouzou and either her parents didn't have the time to focus on what that was, or they had no idea what to do about it.

Laurent would lay odds on the latter.

"I love scrambled eggs, Papa," Mila said as Laurent plated up a small portion for her and tucked in a little scoop of raspberries next to it. He pulled croissants out of the oven. He'd bought them in Aix two days earlier but they warmed up fine for one more day.

"Me, too," Jemmy said. "I thought you were going to teach me to cook? Why is Zouzou learning?"

Laurent slid Jemmy's plate in front of him.

"Less talk," he said which he knew the boy would correctly interpret as *less complaining*.

"Oh, my goodness! Something smells lovely!" Elspeth said as she came down the stairs. Unlike the children she was dressed for the day, wearing an emerald green gabardine pantsuit.

"*Bon matin*, Elspeth," Laurent said, turning back to Zouzou who was seated next to Jemmy, her breakfast in front of her. Laurent couldn't help but see how she hesitated to pick up her fork. Forcing away his annoyance at Windsor and Grace, he put a buttery croissant on her plate.

"Can we have hot chocolate too, Papa?" Mila asked.

"*Bien sûr*," he said as he picked up a ceramic pitcher of hot chocolate he'd made earlier and poured each of the children their hot drinks.

"Just coffee for me," Elspeth said as she moved into the kitchen and poured a cup from the French press.

"And John?" Laurent asked as he removed the toast from the oven and piled it on a plate with a wedge of the creamery butter and set it on the counter, Elspeth sat at the counter and reached for the toast. Laurent handed her a knife.

"He's sleeping in this morning," she said. "Have you heard from Maggie?"

Laurent touched his hands to his shirt pocket although he knew his phone wasn't there.

"Papa still can't find his phone," Jemmy said and he and Zouzou giggled.

"Has she called you?" Laurent asked Elspeth.

Elspeth moved into the living room to get her purse. She fed Petit-Four a corner of toast and the dog followed her back into the kitchen where she handed Laurent her phone.

There was nothing from Maggie.

"Would you have expected to hear from her by now?" Laurent asked, wrinkling his brow.

"No. I would imagine she'd only contact you."

Laurent quickly typed in a text on Elspeth's phone: <*can't find my phone (this is Laurent) call me as soon as you get this message so I know you're alive>*

"May I keep your phone for the day?" he asked.

"Of course." Elspeth turned to the children. "So what are we going to do today, my darlings? How about a game of *Find Daddy's Phone*?"

All three children laughed.

Laurent glanced at the screen of Elspeth's phone with Maggie's photo on it and he felt his heart catch. It wasn't normal for Maggie not to call. If not to talk with him, then to the children.

"Can we watch TV, Papa?" Jemmy asked as he jumped down from his kitchen stool.

"*Non*," Laurent said. "Go play outside."

"It's freezing outside!"

"It's warm in the kitchen if you want to do the dishes."

"I'll get my coat," Jemmy said. "Are you coming too, Z?"

"Sure." Zouzou glanced at Laurent. "I need to burn off that hot chocolate."

It bothered Laurent to hear her say that but he knew whatever was wrong with Zouzou would not be fixed so easily.

As the children scampered away, Elspeth turned to Laurent, a grave expression on her face.

"Have you thought more about what I said to you?" she asked.

Laurent began stacking the dirty dishes in the sink.

"Laurent? We need to talk about this. John is getting worse by the minute."

"Have you talked to Maggie about what you want her to do?" he asked.

"I told her I needed her at home."

"And what did she say?"

"I got the impression that she was wide open to doing exactly that."

"Really."

"I also got the impression that if there was any impediment to her doing that it would likely come from your side."

Laurent knew Elspeth was, as the Americans say, spit-balling. While he had no trouble believing Maggie knew of her mother's wishes and had yet to share them with him, he did not believe she would lead her mother to believe he was the problem.

"Laurent?" she said insistently. "I really must have an answer."

Laurent looked through the window over the sink to the front drive. He saw Mila and Jemmy playing with a ball in the small patch of snow-covered lawn by the gravel driveway. A few hot-house tulips he'd picked up at the flower market in Aix framed the window in two tall glass jars.

For so long it had never occurred to him that this view and this place wasn't forever. That the two children he saw playing on the grounds wouldn't some day turn into grandchildren with he and Maggie growing old together—a part of the *terroir*, a part of the community. His body felt cold and he rubbed the heel of his palm against his chest.

"If Maggie believes we should go back, we will go back," he said flatly, his back still to Elspeth.

The sound of a skateboard dropping onto the hard tiles made Laurent turn to see Zouzou standing in the doorway to the kitchen, her face reddening with outrage.

"You said I could stay and now you're leaving?" she said, her eyes flashing and filled with tears. "I hate you! Your word is no good. Just like Mom's!"

"Calm down, child," Elspeth said, reaching a hand out to her. "We were just talking—"

Zouzou slapped Elspeth's hand away and turned and ran upstairs to her room.

Merde, Laurent thought as he leaned one hip against the stone sink and crossed his arms.

"I can talk with her if you like?" Elspeth said but Laurent shook his head.

"I will go to her once she has settled down," he said.

Elspeth cleared her throat and stood up, looking uncomfortable, even guilty. She went to where her coat hung by the door. "I think I'll just go see how the children are doing," she said and slipped out the front door.

Laurent let out a long sigh and pulled out Elspeth's phone.

John was Maggie's father. Maggie had to be the one to decide. And *he* had to make that decision as easy for her as he could. That much he knew.

He punched in the phone number from memory and waited until the property agent picked up. Then he outlined briefly the terms by which he would be selling Domaine St-Buvard.

The agent responded excitedly, "That will be no problem, Monsieur Dernier."

"*Bon*," Laurent said in a flat voice, his arms feeling leaden and numb. "Come back to me with an offer."

Once he disconnected, Laurent looked around the kitchen. The dirty pans, the half-eaten plates of scrambled eggs, the cold coffee left thickening into grounds in the French press. He felt a heaviness in his shoulders at the thought that someday this would no longer be his. He shook off the sensation. It was indulgent and helped nothing.

Just as he was about to head for the stairs and Zouzou, he heard Jemmy shout from outside and he glanced out the window. A police car was slowly edging up the drive, obviously being mindful of the children. Laurent recognized the car as belonging to Roger Bedard, the *Commandant de Police* in the province west of Aix-en-Provence which included St-Buvard.

At the time Laurent had met Maggie, he'd been making his living as a con man working all the wealthy villages up and down the Côte d'Azur. While he and Bedard had not known each other then, Laurent had no doubt the policeman was aware of Laurent's background.

Remarkably, in spite of that—and the fact that the man was in love with Maggie—he and Bedard had become friends.

But Laurent couldn't remember a time when Bedard had just dropped by for a visit.

Laurent went to the front door and swung it open. Bedard was on the doorstep.

"I've been trying to get through to you for hours," Bedard said, his face pinched and tense. "Have you not seen the news?"

Laurent felt himself rocking slightly on the balls of his feet as a sudden spike of nascent fear erupted deep in his gut. There was a sour taste in his mouth as he waited for Bedard to speak.

"There's been an accident," Bedard said.

25

A WHITER SHADE OF HELL

M aggie felt a sudden coldness hit her at her core at Alys's words and for a moment she felt disoriented.
Manon is missing too?

What could this mean?

Did Grace and Manon leave together? Did Manon lure Grace away? Was Manon hiding some place plotting to kill off the rest of them one by one?

Maggie shuffled back to the same table she had shared with Grace. There were tablecloths on the carpet and she knelt now and picked up the one she thought Grace had used. Under the scent of harsh laundry soap, she could just barely detect the floral notes of *Je Reviens*, Grace's signature perfume.

"Madame?" Max said as he approached her. "You are not seeing anything in the kitchen?"

Again, Maggie was assailed with the growing belief that Max was a little too interested in what she had or hadn't seen in the kitchen.

Without answering him, she turned to face the others. Serge was sitting on the floor, his arm around Lisa.

"Monsieur Tourielle," Maggie said to him. "Your wife was sleeping by your side. You didn't see her get up?"

Maggie knew it was entirely possible he hadn't. After all, Grace had been sleeping only an arm's distance from *her* and Maggie hadn't seen her get up either. So she was surprised by Serge's answer.

"Yes, I saw her," Serge said. "In fact, she told me she was leaving."

Maggie felt a sudden weariness and sat down heavily on the nearest chair as the rest of the group gasped in surprise at Serge's words.

"And you just let her go?" Max said incredulously. He shook his head as if he couldn't believe any husband would do such a stupid thing.

But Maggie believed it. Serge's marriage was over. Unless he was lying about everything he'd probably long ago crossed over into the *whatever-you-say-dear* stage of living with Manon. The fact that he had a mistress probably said all anyone needed to know about how much Serge cared for Manon's safety. So him keeping her secret didn't surprise Maggie a bit.

"Has she been taken do you think?" Alys said, biting her lip. "Who would do such a thing?"

"Why not the man who was cheating on her?" Max said as he stared at Serge.

"Look," Maggie said. "We don't know for sure that Manon or Grace have been harmed. They might just have—"

"What are you accusing me of?" Serge said angrily to Max. "Why would I want to hurt Manon? If I wanted to be rid of her I could just divorce her!"

"Well, why haven't you?" Lisa asked sullenly.

"What about *you*?" Raj said to Max. "I saw you and Madame Toureille last night shagging in the linen closet."

Serge gasped and turned to gape at Max.

"That is a lie," Max said, his eyes darting to Alys.

"I don't believe it!" Serge said vehemently.

"Why do you care who Manon is sleeping with?" Lisa asked him, her face contorted into furious lines.

"I *don't* care!" Serge said, glaring at Max. "But it is an affront to Manon to have such lies told of her behind her back."

"Everyone, stop!" Maggie said in frustration. She turned to Serge. "What did your wife say to you before she left?"

"She said she refused to die buried in this grave," Serge said. "Her exact words. *Enterré dans cette tombe.* She said she would come back with help. If you knew my Manon, you would not doubt her ability to do precisely that."

"*Your* Manon?" Lisa said stridently, flinging Serge's arm off her. Her face was flushed and her facial muscles were twitching. Things were bad for everyone at this point but for some reason they were particularly bad for Lisa. Something was wrong with her.

Maggie was about to suggest that they all come together in a circle and one person at all times remain awake when both the Patels approached them. Maggie was surprised to see that Raj had his arm around Aishwarya's shoulders but somehow it looked more of a show of possession than actual protection.

Maggie rubbed her eyes and admonished herself for the thought. It was only her habit of seeing things a certain way because she'd already made up her mind about people.

"Excuse me," Raj said loudly and stared at Maggie expectantly.

"Yes, Raj? What is it?" Maggie said tiredly. She saw him frown at the use of his first name but she didn't have the energy for all the European civilities at the moment.

"My wife needs to use the facilities," Raj said. "I would escort her there myself of course but—"

"No," Maggie said. "I don't think any of the men should leave this room until we're rescued. And anyone needing to use the facilities will be escorted. No more solo trips anywhere."

Her heart squeezed painfully at the thought of Grace. The rule was too late for Grace. Maggie turned to Alys and handed her the flashlight.

"Will you take her?" Maggie said. "I need someone to retrace my steps to see if I missed anything."

"I will go with you, *chérie*," Max said immediately, further ratcheting up Maggie's fear that he knew more than he should about what happened to Grace.

"No, Max," Alys said, before Maggie could. "Your step is too heavy. I will do it." She took the flashlight and squared her shoulders with resolution.

As Maggie watched the exchange between Max and Alys she thought again that perhaps the two were closer than they wanted people to know. If Alys was sleeping with LeFleur, that gave Max motive for killing the chef. But if Max really had had a dalliance with Manon, then that gave Alys a motive for killing *her*.

As Aishwarya and Alys made their way through the dining room to the hall, Raj seated himself at Maggie's table and drummed the tabletop impatiently with his fingernails.

"As for the rest of us," Maggie said, turning to Max, Serge and Lisa—who now sat with her arms crossed on her chest, a glowering expression on her face, "I think we should all try to stay awake. I would hate to miss the sound of our rescuers because I think every minute counts at this point."

"You are thinking the oxygen is depleting?" Max said.

"I was thinking more of the ceiling is falling," Maggie said. *That and the fact that somebody among us is trying to kill us off one by one.*

"I for one will have a long and emphatic complaint about how this catastrophe was handled," Raj said to no one in particular

"Nobody cares what you think," Max said.

Raj, who had been leaning back in his chair with the front

legs off the carpet, brought the chair down hard on the floor to face Max.

"You *will* care, you cretin," he said menacingly. "When you are looking for a new job at your age!"

Maggie was about to tell them both to shut up when a horrified scream from the hallway ended all argument.

26

A MOMENT IN TIME

Grace felt the nightmare coming to life.

She tried to open her eyes. But still she saw nothing.

With the burgeoning consciousness she felt her stomach roil as the drubbing pain whirled in her skull. The pain came in waves, each more dominant than the last, each more unendurable.

She wet her lips. She was so thirsty, her throat was on fire. She felt the hardness underneath her. It was cold. She tried to push the agony in her head to the background to focus on her surroundings.

Her foot inched out and touched something hard. A wall. She moved her hand and touched another wall. She was in a small space. A coffin. Fighting down the panic that that thought brought, she widened her eyes, hoping they might adjust, but it was hopeless.

There was only complete blackness everywhere.

"Help," she croaked softly. She listened but the sound of the rushing blood pounding in her ears was all she could hear.

She moved her foot again against the wall and her muscles, viciously cramping, screamed at her to stop.

Where am I? What happened?

"Grace? Are you there?"

She smelled him seconds before she heard his voice. It was his aftershave. The scent of it more powerful and insistent than if it had only been yesterday she'd smelled it on him.

"Win...Windsor?" she whispered.

"What have you done, Grace?" he said.

"Where are you?" she said more loudly, her eyes watering from the incessant, relentless pummeling in her head. "I need help."

"That's you all over, isn't it?" the voice said in disgust.

"Windsor, no," she whimpered. "I'm in trouble."

"You know this is for the best, right? For everyone? You, dead?"

"Am...am I dead?" she said, not sure if she'd only thought the words.

"Would I be here in this dungeon under a mountain of snow and ice if you were alive?"

"I'm...dead?" A feeling of hopelessness filtered through her. She wasn't going to see the girls again? She wasn't going to be able to fix things with Maggie? Grace felt an ache in her chest and a sensation of the world slowing down.

"It's for the best," Windsor said. "Go to sleep now, Gracie."

"Windsor, no," she said. "Please don't leave."

But her words only met silence. She tried to imagine she could still detect his scent. The leather and musk he always wore. But the intensity with which she tried only made her head hurt worse. She couldn't smell it any more. He was gone.

She lifted her head off the ground, sending shock waves of agony riddling through her skull.

Windsor, come back. Please.

She lowered her head again to the cold hard ground and let

the pain in her head envelop her, let it wrack her body, do its worst. She felt herself slipping away from her body, felt her conscious self lift up and step outside her corrupted, corporeal form.

And when she did, the pain eased and then stopped. She remembered a sunny afternoon in Provence so many years ago but it felt like it was happening right now. She and Windsor sat at an outdoor café table, the sun creating dazzling patchworks of shade all around them from the towering plantain trees they sat under. The rosé wine was cold and refreshing. Their Niçoise salads were untouched as they gazed into each other's eyes and marveled that life could be so good.

A sob caught in her throat and she was catapulted back into her body. The ground was rock hard, the cold once more relentlessly drilling up into her hips and shoulders.

Begging for unconsciousness, she tried one last time to remember Windsor's scent and all the lovely times in her life when that scent had always been in the background. When Taylor was born. When they finished the house in Provence. When Zouzou was born and Windsor said he loved Grace so much that he didn't care who the real father was.

Until he did.

She filled her nostrils with the damp smell of cold and mildew, her chest rattling with her efforts to bring Windsor back through his scent when suddenly she found herself remembering another scent. A floral perfume. Roses...and jasmine.

She opened her eyes at the realization. She'd smelled it seconds before she was attacked.

Yes! Her heart quickened as she remembered. She'd followed someone to the bathroom and saw her...*saw who?*

Grace felt her excitement war with the now undeniable pull of the darkness that wanted to reclaim her. She felt the prospect of the relief from her pain beckoning her.

To not feel this agony anymore...

The perfume had been there—faint but definite—and then she'd felt the explosion ricocheting around inside her head and everything had swum away into darkness.

That perfume. I know it. I know who wears it.

A fissure of excitement flared in her chest.

She tried to wrap her mind around the name. But the lure of the taunting relief from the cold and pain was too great. It was winning. It was dragging her back under.

I need to tell Maggie, she thought as she closed her eyes and felt her harsh surroundings begin to drift away.

But before the darkness reached out to take her back to a place warm and safe, her last confused thought came to her and then fluttered away like fog in the wind.

I need to tell Maggie.

I know who the killer is.

27

BLOWING AWAY

A t first Maggie couldn't understand what she was seeing. She and Raj and Max rushed out of the dining room to the hall and the source of the screaming to find Alys and Aishwarya clutching each other in hysteria.

Aishwarya pointed a shaking finger to the long wall opposite the hall. Before Maggie even turned her head to look she knew what she would find.

And she knew she should have looked there first.

There in the fish tank—its broken glass at least half way down its sides and the water long since spilled out into the hall where it saturated the carpet and ran down the hall—was the body.

Twisted and hunched over, the face was turned mercifully away above the pink Hermès scarf Maggie had last seen around Manon's neck.

"Max," Maggie said breathlessly, "take Alys and Aishwarya back to the dining room. Be careful not to touch anything."

For a moment nobody moved or spoke. They all just stared at the terrible sight of the body bent unnaturally, the scarf floating like silken seaweed on the surface of the foot of water still left in the tank. Then Alys and Aishwarya began to shuffle down the hall and Max reached out to take Alys's arm. His mouth open, Raj stared at the fish tank until Maggie gave him a gentle push.

"See to your wife," she said.

Perhaps because he was in shock, he nodded and turned back toward the dining room.

By the time Maggie returned to the dining room, the hysteria there was at a fever pitch. The Patels stood together, although not touching. Aishwarya shook and Raj raged.

Lisa had pulled herself to her feet and stood clutching the edge of a dining table while Alys spoke quietly to Serge—no doubt delivering the news about Manon.

Max leaned against one of the tables, a bottle in one hand and no pretense about needing a glass for it.

The noise level was creeping up higher and higher and Maggie knew that not only were they in danger of the volume unsettling the beams they depended on to keep the weight of the roof off them, but there was no way now that they would hear any sounds of rescue efforts.

"*Mais non!*" Serge shouted. "This cannot be! I must see for myself!" Serge grabbed his head as if assailed by a terrible headache and bent over moaning. He made no move to go to the hallway but stood at the table clutching his arms and shaking.

Maggie rebuked herself for not looking at the aquarium when she'd gone looking for Grace earlier. It hadn't even occurred to her to look at the fish tank.

"Look at his feet!" Lisa shrieked as she pointed to Serge's shoes. "His shoes are wet!"

There was a wet spot where Serge was standing. In the back of her mind Maggie thought she remembered seeing it before and just assumed he'd spilled one of the water pitchers.

"How did he get his feet wet?!" Lisa said.

"What are you saying, *chérie?*" Serge asked as he dropped his hands from his head and stared at her. "You are not well. You don't know what you are saying."

"Why are his feet wet?" Lisa insisted. "If he wasn't in the hall with the broken fish tank? Answer me that!"

Was Lisa saying she thought Serge killed Manon?

"He fought with the chef at breakfast! " Lisa said rancorously, "He told LeFleur he wouldn't be able to get a job at McDo's. Didn't you, Serge?" Her eyes were glassy and half-lidded.

"She doesn't know what she is saying," Serge said helplessly, now openly appealing to the listening group.

"You're all barking," Raj said. "It makes more sense that the idiot ski instructor killed Madame Toureille because he was sleeping with her and was afraid she'd cause a scene like she did with you!"

"*C'est ridicule,*" Max said, slurring his words a little. It wasn't until then that Maggie realized Max was at least a little drunk. He stood and pointed a finger at Maggie.

"Why is her friend missing but there is no body?" he said. "It is because it was *she* who killed LeFleur and also Madame Toureille."

"Actually that is not a ridiculous idea," Alys said turning to Maggie, her eyes narrowing.

"Yes. Please explain why your friend's body is not found," Serge said, staring at Maggie.

Suddenly Lisa slid from her seat and toppled to the floor. Serge made a startled choking sound and knelt beside her, pulling her upright again. She tried to push away his hands but Maggie could see that in spite of the chill in the room she was sweating heavily.

"She's ill," Maggie said, stepping closer to her. "Lisa? What's wrong?"

"Nothing!" Lisa said weakly. "Don't try to distract us!"

But now everyone was staring at Lisa and it was clear the last thing she was, was fine.

"*Chérie*," Serge said. "What can I do to help you? Is it your foot?"

"Stop it! No! All right!" Lisa said in frustration, wiping her hand across her face. "It's my insulin. I need my insulin. Happy now?" She glowered at Serge.

"Insulin?" Maggie said.

"Yes, insulin!" Lisa said, looking at Serge, her bottom lip trembling. "I need insulin."

Maggie ran a hand across her face. *What happens if she doesn't get insulin? Does she go into cardiac arrest? Will she die?* Maggie didn't dare ask and she didn't dare ask how long she could go without it.

What difference did it make? Just like with the possibility of the ceiling caving in, if help didn't come in time *knowing* wouldn't matter.

"Why are the rescuers not here?" Raj said angrily. "Are they not coming? Do the stupid French not even know what has happened?"

"The French know what is happening!" Max growled at him, and then began to slide off the table as if to approach him before catching himself clumsily.

"Stop all of this!" Alys said, clapping her hands. When she did, a piece of ceiling in the far corner cracked and fell in a large thump to the carpet below, burying a table in electrical wires and jagged wood planks from the floor above.

Aishwarya and Lisa both screamed. Lisa clutched at Serge who put his arms around her. Aishwarya reached for Raj but he dusted off her attempts as if she were so much dog hair on his suit.

"We all need to calm down," Maggie said, her heart pounding in her ears. "*No* loud noises. No moving around if you don't have to."

"But of course *you* would say this!" Alys said, her voice shaking with fear. "If it was *you* who has done all this!"

Maggie took a deep breath and opted not to answer. It was such an absurd statement that it was only evidence of how frantic and desperate everyone was feeling at the moment.

Max stared drunkenly at Maggie. "I saw her fight with Denis just before dinner," he said.

"That is not true," Maggie said, feeling a sensation of foreboding crawl up her arms.

"I saw you!" he boomed loudly. Another piece of the ceiling nearer to them now rained down on them, dropping chunks of plaster and molding. Aishwarya yelped and reached again for Raj who was focused on the ceiling and allowed it.

Whether it was the ceiling falling down on them or the accusations she had no answer for or just the overbearing agony of Grace's mysterious disappearance, Maggie felt she couldn't breathe. Perspiration formed on her top lip and when she wiped it off she noticed her hands were trembling.

She couldn't stay here a moment longer. She got to her feet and picked up a flashlight, holding it in two hands in case she needed to use it for a purpose other than just light.

"I'm going to look for Grace in the kitchen again," she said, her eyes going to Max. If he truly had something to hide in there, this should trigger something.

It did.

But not in the way Maggie expected.

"No!" Alys shouted. "Stop her, Max!"

The ski instructor stepped into Maggie's path, his arms stretched out to block her. Maggie felt the panic building in her chest.

She had to get *out* of here.

Without knowing she was going to do it she swung the flashlight at Max's face.

He jerked his head back. Even drunk, his reflexes were good

enough to avoid the hit. Fury flared in his eyes when he realized what she'd tried to do and he lunged for her before she had a chance to cock her arm to try again.

He tackled her and they came down hard in a tangle of legs, knocking the air out of Maggie. Her chest felt like it was exploding and she gasped frantically to bring air into her lungs.

"You are going nowhere, Madame!" Max grunted, his alcohol-laden breath blasting into her face. He slid off her just enough so the weight of him was not fully on her but still pinning her underneath him.

"Hold her, Max!" Alys said. "She killed Denis and Manon! We must hold her until we are rescued."

"No!" Raj said. "If we try to keep her alive, she'll find a way to escape!"

"What are you suggesting?" Aishwarya said in a horrified gasp.

Their words swirled in Maggie's head as she fought for her breath, her arms useless and pinned to her sides.

"Kill her!" Serge shouted. "Before she kills us too!"

No, no, no, Maggie thought, her chest heaving with panic and fear. She had to find Grace before it was too late! Her ears seemed to reverberate with the hum of hysterical voices and with her own terror before she realized she was hearing something else.

Something much worse.

The relentless creaking of the beams overhead had increased and amplified.

Squirming desperately under Max, Maggie saw over his shoulder the moment the ceiling let go.

28

THE DARK SIDE

The thundering sound of the ceiling as it crashed down upon them was unholy and all encompassing, expanding in volume to fill every crack of sensation that Maggie had left. She felt Max's body shudder and then press heavily into her until she couldn't take a single ragged breath.

Alys and Aishwarya screamed and the deadly, ominous cracking sounds of the picture window continued more loudly than before. Using every ounce of strength she had left, Maggie squirmed out from under Max—now a leaden, lifeless weight on top of her. Her heart was pounding as she scooted away from him, boards and ceiling plaster everywhere around her. A heavy beam rested on Max's neck.

In the darkness Maggie saw flecks of plaster floating in the air like powered milk. Looking up where the ceiling used to be she saw only a cavern of inky black.

"Is...everyone okay?" she asked hoarsely and began coughing. She reached out to find Max's pulse in his neck and after a moment inched further away from him. Max was never going to be okay ever again.

"What happened?" Alys said shrilly. "Did the ceiling collapse? Max? Are you there?"

Maggie groped around in the dark until she found the flashlight she'd dropped when Max tackled her. She clutched it to her chest and felt a wave of comfort just holding it. Her relief was short lived.

The room was much colder than it had been just seconds before—almost as if there was now an opened channel somewhere to the outside. While it was the broken beams overhead that had taken down the ceiling—or most of it from what Maggie could see when she played the flashlight beam upward—it was the weight of the snow on the roof that was the real worry now.

Once that broke through, they would all suffocate.

Then it wouldn't matter if the first responders were in the next room about to break through or still drawing up their coordinates in the next village. It would be too late. They would all be dead.

"Lisa! Lisa!" Serge cried. "Wake up! Somebody help me! She is unconscious!"

Maggie knew there was nothing they could do for Lisa. But Serge's panicking was making everything worse. She struggled to her feet and pointed the light around the room until she spotted everyone.

The ceiling had come down furthest from the window revealing that the one place they thought they were the safest was actually the most deadly.

We couldn't have known, Maggie thought miserably, glancing back at Max.

"Max!" Alys shrieked. "Answer me!"

"Stop screaming," Maggie said coldly. "Max was killed when the ceiling came down. And the ceiling came down because you were all making too much noise."

That probably wasn't true but Maggie felt no guilt for saying it. Every person here had done their best to make surviving as difficult as possible. She was seconds away from letting all of them fend for themselves.

The sound of Alys's weeping was soft and unremitting.

"This is all your fault, Raj!" Aishwarya's voice came to Maggie high and reedy. "This whole nightmare is because of you!"

Maggie was surprised but glad to see a little bit of steel in Aishwarya.

It probably won't help much in the long run. But you never know.

"How dare you speak to me like that?" Raj said angrily. The two of them were huddled on the carpet next to Serge and Lisa. The Indian man jerked away from his wife and then viciously backhanded Aishwarya. Maggie saw the woman's head bounce off a table leg.

Fury pumped into Maggie and she pushed a chunk of ceiling debris aside until she stood in front of the couple.

"What is your problem, you little worm?" Maggie said, gripping the flashlight as if she might begin beating the man with it at any moment. "*No* hitting people! Unless you want to take me on!"

"How dare you address me in this manner?" Raj said, his face mottled red with indignation. "She is my wife!"

"Get away from her before I lodge this up your nose!" Maggie said, waving the flashlight at him. "Do you hear me? *Get!*"

Raj hurriedly moved a few feet away from his wife.

"Are you all right, Aishwarya?" Maggie asked.

Aishwarya nodded but looked fearfully at Raj. Maggie knew she'd probably just made things a hundred times worse for the woman. She felt a sudden and powerful wave of exhaustion.

Where was help? Why hadn't someone come for them yet?

Maggie didn't know what time it was any more but she knew the rescue was taking way too long.

"Madame Chaix," Maggie said to Alys. "Make an effort to pull yourself together. These people need your help."

Because I am officially done with all of you.

Sniffing, Alys turned to look at Serge and Lisa. She then pulled a tablecloth from a nearby table and handed it to Serge to drape around Lisa. The author was unconscious. Maggie wasn't a medical expert but she was pretty sure Lisa wasn't going to wake up on her own. She needed insulin.

If it wasn't already too late.

Thinking of things that were too late, Maggie flashed back to her short answers to Grace during this trip, and to the cold silence on the train ride to the chalet. In her mind she saw Grace's hopeful face every time they met—and she remembered her cold resistance in response to it.

It wasn't even about not wanting to be friends anymore. It was always about making her pay for the pain she caused me. I was punishing her.

And now she's gone.

Maggie held out hope that Grace was still alive. But whatever had happened to her—Grace's silence and failure to reappear spoke volumes as to the likelihood that she was still breathing. Maggie pushed the thought from her mind.

Another chunk of the ceiling fell from inside the kitchen and everyone screamed, even Maggie. The strained creaking sound of more beams at their limit echoed into the room from the kitchen. That room would be swamped in minutes, Maggie was sure. It was a miracle it had lasted this long.

Where were the damn rescuers?

Now they knew there was no place in the dining room that was safe. Any part of the rest of the ceiling could come down at anytime, anywhere. And there was still the black mass pressing in on the window—the relentless, pernicious snow wanting in, and the cracking window that would give way any time.

Maggie clutched the flashlight tightly in her hands and saw that its light was much weaker than it had been. If the rescuers didn't come soon they would all be plunged into darkness.

If the rest of the falling ceiling didn't kill them first.

And what about the murders? Was that finished? Was the killer dead?

If the chef had seen something he shouldn't have and was killed, if the detective had taken the poisoned food meant for someone else, if Manon had been the intended victim all along—then they were in the clear and there would be no more killing.

But if any of that was wrong and those murdered people had all been slain randomly, then they very likely still had a killer among them who maybe wasn't done killing.

A chill shot up Maggie's spine and she rubbed a tired hand across her face.

But who?

Max was the most likely suspect and now that he was dead, they could probably all relax.

But what about Serge? He was also a possible suspect for everyone's death.

Alys? Raj? Lisa? Aishwarya?

Only Grace didn't fit into the equation. Why would anyone kill her? And where was her body? None of the others even knew Grace. Killing her just didn't make sense.

Maggie shook her head in exhaustion and felt the bruising on her hips from being tackled to the floor by Max just moments before.

Where are you, Laurent? she thought hopelessly, tears gathering in her eyes. *Do you know I'm in trouble? Are you trying to get to me?*

Just as she was about to sit down on one of the chairs—just to relax for a moment before she left again to search for Grace—she saw a scrap of paper that she'd glimpsed earlier but thought was just part of the debris from the fallen ceiling.

Now as she stared at it she could see it was a folded note.

Maggie leaned over and picked up the paper scrap. She

glanced around to see if anyone was watching her and then opened it up and directed her flashlight beam onto the hand scrawled words.

You will all pay

29

THE COLOR OF FEAR

Blades of icy wind cut through Laurent's jacket and he felt a trail of chilling sleet find its way down his collar where he stood, blinking away snowflakes from his lashes.

The road to the chalet had been completely blocked by a mountain of snow when the avalanche hit.

Laurent now stood in the road, the wet snow pouring out of the sky and whipping around him as he stared at the monster impasse. The air was crisp and so cold it burned his nostrils. Roger Bedard stood next to him.

"How could this have happened?" Laurent murmured, his mind racing.

"Don't go there," Bedard said. "Focus on what we know." The detective shivered and pulled his jacket tighter.

Beside them were two ambulances, parked and ready—but with no way to get where they needed to go. Another two dozen rescuers were milling around the ambulances or huddled in cars talking on communication devices.

"What is that?" Laurent asked numbly. What facts did they know except for the important one that Maggie was trapped in a two hundred year old building under five tons of snow and very likely dead?

"A couple returning from dinner was found trapped in their car," Bedard said. "They said they saw the avalanche swallow up the chalet."

Laurent ran a hand through his hair.

"And so the rescuers have just been sitting here all night?" He looked around in frustration.

"They can't do much else until either the weather clears or we get through this wall of ice."

"Have they *tried*?" Laurent gestured to the pair of snowmobiles parked in front of the impasse.

"You can't go where there is no path," Bedard said reasonably. "We have to drill through this first or go around but going around will take as long as waiting for the weather to let up so the choppers can get in. And even if the choppers can get airborne, they likely won't be able to land."

Laurent felt his clothing growing heavier by the moment as the wet snow soaked through his jeans.

"There has to be a plan besides just wait," he said in frustration.

Bedard hesitated and Laurent turned to him.

"What is it?" Laurent asked. "What do you know?"

"They have infrared equipment that they'll use to pinpoint locations once we get closer to see where any survivors would be."

"*Any survivors*? What aren't you saying?"

Bedard pinched his lips together and shook his head vehemently. "The couple that witnessed the avalanche barely escaped with their lives. They said they saw the snow eat the chalet, crushing everything as flat as a crepe. They are telling the rescuers that there is no way anyone could have survived it." Bedard's voice dropped and Laurent heard a hint of a tremble in it.

"She's alive," Laurent said. "I cannot believe she's not alive."

"I know."

The communication device on Bedard's collar crackled and he turned away to speak into it. When he came back, he gestured for Laurent to follow him to one of the ambulances. An EMT sat shielding himself from the downpour of flurries, a thermos of coffee in his hands.

"Any more of that?" Bedard nodded at the hot drink. The man turned and found two mugs which he poured coffee into and handed to Laurent and Bedard.

Laurent followed Bedard to his police cruiser by the line of fir trees that fringed the road leading to the village of Valmeinier and Grenoble proper. He hated wasting a single moment when they could be digging through that monster ice blockage but he took his seat in Bedard's car.

"Well?"

"A couple things," Bedard said. "First, they think they've found a way around the impasse."

Laurent felt his sense heighten at Bedard's words. He rubbed his hands together.

"*However*," Bedard said firmly. "It's possible that once they start around they'll just find another impasse. That's already happened twice so far. And going around will take time. Hours, possibly longer."

"I want to go with them."

"I knew you would say that, but Laurent, you need to let the professionals do this. We only have two snowmobiles and we need them to be manned by emergency rescue personnel. You see that, right?"

Cursing Bedard's sound logic, Laurent turned to watch the snow coat the outside of the car window. Through the window he could see only a screen of opaque white, whirling and spinning.

"You said a couple of things," Laurent said.

"I'm not sure how important they are," Bedard said.

"Tell me."

"The mother of one of the chalet's guests says her daughter is seriously diabetic. If she doesn't get her insulin, she'll die. If she isn't able to get to it—"

"Yes, yes," Laurent said impatiently. "Is that all?"

"We've received word that another of the guests was recently released from a mental hospital," Bedard said. "I didn't write her name down but it seems this guest made death threats against several people just in the last few days since her release."

"So she is unbalanced," Laurent said.

"Her doctor said murderously so."

"Then why the hell was she released?"

"That I do not know."

"*Bon.* So Maggie is buried under a hundred tons of snow with a dying diabetic woman and a crazed murderer. Is that all?"

"No, one more thing."

"*Mon Dieu,*" Laurent said, rubbing a large hand over his face. "What?"

"It's possible that once they make it to the avalanche site that attempting to dig them out will cause either another avalanche or cause the already brittle and ancient beams of the chalet to collapse."

30

DREAM ON

The sound of the explosion jolted Grace to consciousness. Her ears were ringing. She had the sensation of trying to hold back a scream that wouldn't be stopped.

The ceiling was coming down.

She froze and held her breath, listening to the creaking beams above her grew louder and louder. Dust and debris rained down and left her gasping for breath.

Something felt different about her space.

She moved her foot but the wall was gone. She felt a flutter in her stomach as she allowed hope to infuse her in spite of the strident creaking sounds of the walls.

She lifted her head slowly off the floor and felt an immediate pulsating nausea slam into her. Her head spun and the dizziness left her gasping as she lowered her head back down and waited for the sensation to calm down.

Something dripped into her eye. Blood? She reached up to feel her head when a pain that felt like an axe slamming into her erupted in her arm. She held her breath but the awakened agony soared to the top of her sensations now and would not be coaxed back into acquiescence again. Like a jumping, erratic electrical wire, it raced up and down her forearm in a series of white-hot vibrating shocks.

Don't move, she thought. *Just. Don't. Move.*

The grinding sound of the creaking ceiling sent another shiver of terror through her.

I have to move! I have to get out!

She lay trembling on the floor, trying to control her breath. She licked her lips and suddenly she realized she was lying on a different floor than before. It was still stone and cold but now there was a rug under her.

Did she come back and move me? she thought in bewilderment. *Why not just kill me?*

Desperately, she tried to run through what she knew about her situation. *I'm somewhere totally dark. My arm is hurt. My head is hurt. I'm freezing.*

She swallowed hard and squeezed her eyes shut. Assessing her situation had only made her realize how hopeless it all was.

She felt the wetness on her face again and wondered if her head was still bleeding from the blow she now remembered suffering. But when the saltiness dribbled into her mouth, she realized she was crying.

She was never going to see her children again. She was never going to see them grow up, or see them happy.

She had a grandchild coming.

Her body began to shake from the cold and her horrifying realizations.

Please don't let me die like this, she wept, ignoring the raging pain in her arm as she lay on the cold floor. *Please show me the way out of here. Give me another chance to be a good mother to my girls.*

The abrupt thud as a piece of ceiling fell nearly on top of her made her scream—which jolted her arm and her head—and she lay stunned in vibrating agony for long seconds while the pain slowly went back in its box.

How was she ever going to have the strength to stand up and try to find a way out of where ever she was? In the dark? With a murderer who knows exactly where she is?

She closed her eyes. Maybe Windsor was right. Maybe dying here was the best thing she could do for Taylor and Zouzou. They could have a clean slate with someone else and in time they'd forget her. That would probably be the best thing for everyone.

"Now you're talking," Windsor said.

She hadn't smelled his cologne this time but it didn't matter. She knew it wasn't really him.

"Although I'm surprised you'd leave your new boyfriend so easily."

She deserved that. Windsor was probably a little jealous but he wanted her to know he believed she'd miss her boyfriend before she missed her own children. Yes. She deserved that too.

"He'd have just dumped you anyway. You know that, right?"

What did I ever see in you, Windsor?

"I mean his kids already don't want you in his life and sooner or later he'd see you're too much drama for any normal man."

Normal, like you, Windsor?

"Go to sleep, Grace," Windsor-not-Windsor said. "I'll take care of the girls. They don't need you. Nobody does. Sleep well, darling."

Grace felt Windsor leave and this time she wasn't sorry to be alone. Dying was a private business. She hoped she had time to pray her regrets and her contrition. She'd been terrible about going to church lately but she was pretty sure He still listened to her.

Just a little nap, first, she thought as the darkness came and coaxed away the pain bit by blessed bit.

31

TRUE GRIT

You will all pay
Scrawled in English in an angry black felt tip pen.
Maggie held the flashlight beam, shaking now, and read the words over and over again. The killer was no longer content with just killing his victims, he needed to taunt the survivors now.

Maggie's hand with the note in it fell to her knee.

So. Unless the killer was Max, it's not over.

And it won't be over until they're all dead. And since rescue will likely come within the hour whoever is killing them will need to escalate the plan.

Which means I have to find the killer. I can't wait. I can't quit.

Because he won't.

Maggie looked from face to face at all the people in the room and tried to see the killer in each of them.

Maybe it had been Max? She glanced back at his body. It probably was him. He was the only one with access to the chef. The only one with a motive for killing Manon—that is if he truly had been sleeping with her.

But Maggie couldn't take the chance that it wasn't him. The

message in the note clearly meant that whoever the killer was, he wasn't giving up. And so Maggie couldn't either.

She stood and tucked the note in the pocket of her jeans. If they lived through this, they could at least test the note for the killer's DNA. She picked up a steak knife from a nearby table and slipped it into her back pocket.

"Where are you going?" Alys said. "We are not supposed to leave this room except in pairs."

"Change of plans," Maggie said. "I'm going looking for Grace again and you all are going to stay here in this room. I suggest you don't take your eyes off each other."

Without waiting to hear their reaction, Maggie pushed past a chunk of fallen plaster laced with wires to make her way to the hall and bathrooms. Maybe the ceiling falling had changed the topography where she'd looked last and she'd see something she'd missed.

That sounded desperate even to her ears.

She stood at the opening of the hallway and studied what she was looking at. On the left hand wall the fish tank was completely empty of water now with Manon's body still crumpled inside it. Feeling more than slightly squeamish, Maggie didn't look closely at that for the moment. She tried to take in anything else that might be different, forcing herself to really see the walls, the bathroom door, the sodden carpet...

And that's when she saw it.

Or rather she didn't see what should have been there. Opposite the fish tank was the glass display alcove that had showcased the latest skiwear circa 1962. The glass had been broken by the avalanche but that wasn't what was significant.

There was no longer a mannequin in the display case.

Maggie took several steps toward the case trying to understand what she was seeing. Could the avalanche have swept the mannequin away? But that made no sense. The rest of the display case was unharmed. A pair of ski goggles still rested on the glass shelf next to where the mannequin had been positioned.

Suddenly a feeling came over Maggie that began gradually before racing toward her like an oncoming truck out of control. She turned slowly to look at the fish tank on the opposite wall. And that's when she saw what nobody had wanted to look closely enough to see.

It wasn't Manon's body in the tank. It was the mannequin.

Maggie stumbled over to the fish tank and reached past the glass shards of the broken aquarium walls to touch the rubbery mannequin. It had been twisted over, its face pointed away, and Manon's scarf wrapped around its neck. Once you knew it wasn't real it was hard to see it as anything but fake.

We all saw what we were supposed to see.

Chills raced up Maggie's arms as she realized what must have happened. Manon wanted them to think she was dead.

And there could be only one reason why she would do that.

So she could go on killing.

Suddenly it was so clear to her. Manon must have killed the chef because he caught her in the kitchen poisoning one of the dishes, probably Lisa's.

Manon is the killer.

Maggie tried to rack her brain for the exact moment when she'd first seen Manon come into the dining room.

The rest of them had been there for several minutes. They'd all ordered their meals and had some drinks served. Manon had come in from the direction of the lobby. But there was a conduit from this hall to the kitchen via the men's room. Manon could easily have entered the kitchen unseen in order to poison a dish before being caught by LeFleur.

But *when* had she killed LeFleur? Except for Patel, only Max was in and out of the kitchen and by then Manon had made her big entrance with Serge and there was nobody who'd taken their eyes off her after that. Maybe that was the whole point? From the perspective of an alibi?

Could Manon and Max have been working in tandem?

Manon killed Lisa and Max killed LeFleur and they each provided the other in the way of a diversion for an alibi? That would definitely work if the two of them were lovers as Raj claimed he knew for a fact.

But then why go after Grace?

Unless Grace saw Manon get up in the middle of the night and followed her and was attacked.

It was very likely that Grace had caught Manon red-handed setting up the mannequin in the fish tank and confronted her.

Maggie felt a wave of guilt as she envisioned it. It sounded exactly like something Grace would do. Especially if she were trying to win her way back into Maggie's heart. The two of them, back in the saddle again. Nancy Drew and Beth.

Maggie's eyes pricked with tears and she forced herself not to revisit all the times this week she'd turned away from Grace. She felt a tightness in her chest as she brought the image of Grace to mind—her face smiling and hopeful—only to be dashed by some thoughtless retort or offhand snub from Maggie. She felt the shame of those moments grind deep in her gut.

She tried to shake herself out of her thoughts.

She needed to focus on finding Manon before she killed again. And perhaps, just maybe, Manon hadn't killed Grace yet.

Maggie turned to examine the hallway more closely. It made sense that whatever had happened to Grace had happened around the ladies bathroom. She stopped to listen to hear if anyone was coming from the dining room but the way the hall was configured made it impossible to hear noises coming from there.

Maggie looked down the hall toward the dining room. *So somewhere here*, she thought, scanning the walls and the floor. *Grace confronted Manon and then Manon...what? attacked Grace?* But even if Manon had killed Grace, where was the body? Grace wasn't heavy by any means but she wasn't diminutive either. Plus Manon was smaller than Grace. There was no way she'd be able to shift a dead body.

Maggie ran her hands over the wall, hoping for a secret hatch or something and then spotted a heating grate close to the floor. Her heart beating quickly at her discovery, she dropped to one knee in front of it. The coldness from the drenched floor shocked her for a moment.

This close to the floor, Manon could drag Grace to the grate and push her into it, Maggie thought. The grate opening was narrow but a normal sized woman could squeeze through.

"Grace?" Maggie called through the grate as she pulled the knife out of her pocket to pry the cover plate off before realizing the screws were gone. The cover lifted easily.

A burst of sudden awareness jolted her. She'd found it! There could be no other reason for the screws to be missing than that this conduit had been used recently!

Sliding the cover onto the floor Maggie turned on her flashlight, its beam milky faint. She flashed it into the dark space.

It was wider inside, easily space enough for a full grown man to fit. But it wasn't the surprise of the spaciousness that stunned Maggie.

It was the body she saw inside.

Her heart began to beat in her chest like a kettledrum.

The head of the body was turned away and in the dark, even with her light, Maggie couldn't determine if it was wearing Grace's clothes.

"Grace?" she said again, her voice echoing in the metal tunnel.

There was no answer. The body lay eight feet into the darkened tunnel. Maggie couldn't pull it out without going inside herself. Her stomach churning with dread, Maggie tucked her flashlight back into her pocket, plunging her in darkness once more, and crawled inside.

The space slanted sharply downward and Maggie had to grip the sides of the tunnel with the crepe soles of her shoes to keep from sliding into the body.

Forcing herself not to think, not to hope, she crawled toward the body. Within a few seconds she was close enough to touch a leg. It was cold.

And sticky wet.

Maggie's heart thundering in her chest and a thousand prayers on her lips, she pulled out her flashlight with shaking hands and army-crawled abreast with the body. She lifted the closest wrist to her and tried to find a pulse.

Nothing.

With tears streaking down her face she braced herself to see the beloved familiar features of her friend. She turned on the flashlight and directed its beam on the face of the corpse.

It was Manon.

32

BEYOND THE EDGE

For a moment, Maggie's emotions surged between joy that the body wasn't Grace's and horror that this meant that Manon was *not* the killer.

She stared at Manon's face and tried desperately to put together what it could mean.

Who had killed Manon? And why?

Suddenly she heard movement behind her in the hallway. It occurred to her that she'd been aware of some undefinable sound for the last several moments but had been so intent on discovering who the body was that her mind had dismissed the noises.

Now she knew what they were.

They were the sounds of screws being tightened against metal.

"Hey!" Maggie yelled. "Hey, I'm in here!"

No one answered.

"Hey! Don't lock me in here! Do you hear me?" She tried to turn around but the space was too narrow so she inched backward on her stomach, her terror mounting. She began to hyperventilate.

When her feet touched the grate she screamed, "Hey! Anybody! Help!"

She heard the sounds of feet squishing in the wet carpet as they hurried away from the grate.

A shiver of terror shimmied through Maggie. For a moment she considered trying to smash the grate with her feet but she couldn't imagine being strong enough to break though metal—and the effort might collapse the tunnel.

She called out again for a few more seconds but she knew no one could hear her from the dining room.

She lay there for a moment, her limbs trembling and her mind whirling trying to imagine who could have done this. Were the footsteps she'd heard heavy or light? A man's or a woman's? But she'd been so focused on letting them know that she was inside the conduit that she couldn't recall. Her fear had camouflaged everything else around her.

Help is coming, she told herself. *Remember that.*

Wasn't it?

But the truth was they should have been rescued hours ago. If help was coming. And if help *wasn't* coming, then she was going to die in a seventeenth century air shaft with a freshly dead body for company.

In a flash, she got an image of Jemmy riding on his father's shoulders through the vineyards. It was that time when she'd been pregnant with Mila on a beautiful late summer day. Laurent had looked so handsome and so happy with the sun on his face. He was owner of a vineyard with a wife he cherished and a son he never thought he'd have. *She* had done that for Laurent. *She* had given him that happy smile.

And she'd be damned if she'd make him a widower before Mila started kindergarten.

She began to crawl back to the corpse, not stopping when she reached it but edging past it.

Didn't these ancient conduits lead to other areas in the chalet? She didn't know but if one way was blocked, she'd just need to find another. She moved quickly, knowing that any second she might find her passage blocked by debris. If she did, she was dead.

She reached the end of the conduit before she knew it was coming. Unlike the grated entrance in the hallway by the dining room, the grate on this end was wooden. She had no idea where it emptied out to but by flashing her light through the wooden trellis cover, she could see it was a room of some kind.

She grabbed the wooden bars of the grate and shook them. She felt one of the bars crack under her fingers and she swiftly twisted around and kicked at the grate. The ceiling of the tunnel was too low to allow her to lift her knees very high to kick with much strength. And she worried that smashing anything too violently would bring the rest of the ceiling down on her. But she had no other options now.

She felt the final kick that did it when she heard the crunch of shattering wood and her feet felt no more resistance. Trembling with excitement and hope, she turned and pulled herself to the ledge of the opening and peered out. Cursing the fact that in her impatience she'd forgotten to use her light, she pulled it out of her pocket and turned it on.

She ran the failing flashlight beam over the room and saw it was a storage room of some kind. The room was small and hemmed in by stacks of crates holding dusty bottles. There was a high window that looked to be level with the ground outside. Being a vintner's wife, Maggie instantly recognized that she'd found the wine cellar. The lone window wasn't much help. Even if she could stack the crates high enough to reach it, the snow on the ground outside the window would make any exit impossible. Her light picked out the shadowy semblance of a door.

The drop to the floor was only about four feet and Maggie could see that the door was accessible by a staircase with a wooden railing. She looked beneath her to make a mental picture of her intended landing spot so that she could hit it when she turned the light off but still see it in her mind's eye. Just as she was about to turn off the light and jump, she heard a noise. She froze.

Rats? she thought unhappily, playing her fading light once more along the storeroom floor among the bottles and crates.

I can deal with rats if I can see them, she thought.

But once her light was gone it would be a different story. And her light would soon be gone. She licked her lips and ran the flashlight beam more slowly around the room—even though she knew she was running down her battery and running out of time.

The noise came again and this time Maggie sucked in a harsh breath.

Not rats. It was a groan.

"Grace?" she said softly, not believing but hoping against hope.

"Help me," a small voice said.

Grace's voice.

33

LIKE A KNIFE IN THE HEART

"Grace!" Maggie shouted, unmindful of the now creaking wooden beams overhead in the wine cellar. "Grace, I'm here!"

She couldn't see where the voice was coming from. Quickly stuffing the flashlight in her pocket, Maggie turned onto her stomach and pushed off the edge until she was hanging on the rim of the conduit by her hands. She let herself drop to the floor below. The flashlight fell out of her pocket with a sound of breaking plastic as it hit the hard stone floor.

She was instantly aware of the drop in temperature.

"Grace?" Maggie said again as she found the flashlight and flicked it back on. The beam swept the small space again. The walls were lined with stacks of wooden crates, the wine bottles on their sides slotted into heavy wooden trellises that flanked the staircase that led to the small wooden door.

Another moan answered her and Maggie directed the light where it had come from.

There, in what looked like a pile of canvas and loosely stacked newspapers, she saw the gleam of a pale face and the golden curls that framed it.

Maggie ran to Grace and dropped to her knees. She sucked in a quick breath when she saw the blood.

"I'm here, sweetie," she said. Grace's eyes fluttered open but she didn't turn in Maggie's direction.

"My head," Grace whispered.

Maggie felt the back of Grace's head. A head wound would bleed a lot, she knew, so she held out hope that maybe all the blood wasn't as bad as it looked. On the other hand, it could hardly be good. She drew her hand away. It was dark red. She wiped her hand on her jeans.

The wound looked as if it had stopped bleeding but she looked around the room for something to wrap around Grace's head. Not finding anything she turned back to Grace and took her pulse. It was erratic but felt strong.

"What happened?" Maggie said. "Who did this to you?"

"Water," Grace croaked, her eyes closing again.

Maggie shrugged out of her wool cardigan—Grace needed it more than she did right now. She draped the sweater over Grace and moved her hands quickly over the rest of Grace's body to detect any other injuries. Grace groaned when Maggie reached her elbow. The arm was at an odd angle. Maggie grimaced. If whoever it was had attacked Grace and pushed her down the heating grate, to end up here in the wine cellar meant that Grace must have crawled to the end—and then fallen into the room. That's probably how she broke her arm.

A head injury, a broken arm and shock.

A loud creak overhead reminded Maggie that those were likely the least of their worries. She figured they were somewhat safer in the cellar than on the floor above but whenever the ceiling caved in completely—as it was threatening to do—it could easily come through to the basement. The overhead beams were not a part of any recent renovations that Maggie could see. They were ancient and crumbling.

"Maggie?"

"Yes, sweetie," Maggie said. "I'm here, Grace." She squeezed Grace's hand and allowed herself to feel a brief moment of joy to have found her alive.

"Back in...business?" Grace said, her eyes still closed, her breathing shallow.

"I think you need to try to stay awake, Grace," Maggie said. "Okay? Can you do that, please?"

Without opening her eyes, Grace gave a faint smile and an imperceptibly small shake of her head.

"Sorry, no," Grace said. "Next...question."

Another creak in the ceiling overhead was followed by a large piece of the ancient beam that barely missed Maggie's knee.

There was no way she was going to be able to get Grace out of here. Not without Grace helping a good deal. But she could at least find something to keep her warm. Spotting a pile of dusty draperies in the corner, Maggie stood up just as her light flickered out for good.

Crap!

Tossing the flashlight aside, Maggie staggered toward the pile of drapes, trying to use the memory picture of where they were in her mind as her guide. She held her hands out in front of her to feel her way. It was closer than she thought and within seconds she had them and was crawling back to Grace.

When she felt with her hands that she'd reached Grace, she unspooled the fabric and draped it on top of Grace.

"Are you awake, Grace?" Maggie asked.

No answer.

Should she stay down here and try to keep her awake? Or go find water and more blankets? Maggie glanced in the direction of where she remembered the stairs were. It was too dark to see them but she knew roughly where they were.

"Maggie?"

"Yes, sweetie, I'm here." Maggie took Grace's hand and warmed it between hers.

"I'm sorry."

Maggie felt a punch of remorse. Was this going to be too late for them? Were they really going to find their way back to each other just to lose each other? Why had Grace's apologies—her abject contrition—been so worthless to Maggie? Why couldn't she have been a decent friend and accepted the first heartfelt apology out of Grace's mouth months ago and moved forward?

A lump formed in Maggie's throat.

"Don't be sorry, Grace," she said. "I'm the one who's sorry."

I'm sorry for being such a spiteful, unrelenting, unforgiving bad excuse of a friend.

"My fault," Grace said, her eyes still closed, her voice sounding like it was underwater now.

"Both our faults," Maggie said, her eyes stinging with tears. "You forgive me and I forgive you."

"Done," Grace said softly, her beautiful lips curled into a soft smile. "Done. And. Done."

It sounded so final that Maggie leaned over and gave her a gentle shake.

"Please don't go to sleep, Grace," she said.

But Grace's head fell gently away from Maggie.

Maggie jumped to her feet and stumbled in the direction of where she remembered the stairs were. She bumped her shins on a table in her path and pushed past it, waving her arms to shield her from anything that might be jutting out at face level. Within six steps she found the rough wooden railing of the stairs.

A shiver of relief rippled through her chest as she gripped the railing and ran up the stairs, one hand in front of her to tell her when she'd reached the top.

She felt for the door handle.

And prayed.

Surely to God if it was locked it wouldn't be locked on the inside?

The door opened.

Relief flooded her and she felt a sudden lightness in her chest as she scanned the room and realized that it was the kitchen. A glow of light from the dining room shot most of the objects into shadow but she could see better than in the wine cellar. A small stool was in arm's reach and she grabbed it and wedged it against the door, propping it open.

Something told Maggie to be quiet.

Something told her not to let the others know where she was.

She moved painstakingly slowly into the kitchen. Without a flashlight she could only make out vague darkened shapes. She could still hear water splashing somewhere on the floor from the burst pipe. She tried to gauge where she was in relation to LeFleur's body. If she was right, she was on the other side of the main prep table. Because she hadn't been able to access it before due to the ceiling debris, she hadn't had an opportunity to search this part of the kitchen.

The last thing she needed to do was go through cupboards and knock something over to alert everyone where she was. While voices and sound didn't carry in the hallway, she wasn't at all sure they wouldn't here in the kitchen. One of the swinging doors to the kitchen had been ripped away in the initial avalanche. That meant anyone in the dining room could see her with a flashlight if they were near the entrance.

Taking a long breath, Maggie inched her way along the counters. She couldn't see far enough ahead of her to know if she was about to run into debris so she had to force herself to go slowly. Gently she eased open the first drawer she came to and ran her hands inside. Silverware.

She held her breath and heard voices which confirmed to her that noises could be heard in the dining room from the kitchen.

If I can hear them, they can hear me too.

She knew one of the people in that room was the killer. One of the people in that dining room had killed LeFleur and Manon. One of the people in that room had tried to kill Grace and had blocked Maggie's access in the heating conduit leaving her to die.

In the second drawer Maggie found a flat plastic box and her heart beat in double time as she ran her fingers over it. Quietly, she pulled it out and set it on the counter and opened it up. Inside she could feel bandage strips, a squeezing tube of some kind of salve and packets of pills. In the dark she had no way of knowing what the pills were but her best guess was that they were some kind of pain medicine. She jammed the packets in her pocket and looked around the kitchen suddenly realizing that unlike the wine cellar, her eyes were growing used to the darkness.

There must be just enough light to aid me in adjusting to it, she thought as she scanned the broken shelves and cupboards nearest to her. She saw nothing of use and was anxious to get back to Grace. As she turned, her foot hit something heavy and she froze. For a moment it sounded as if the hum of conversation in the dining room had stopped.

After a second, she heard a voice—a female voice speaking to the others. *That would have to be Alys*, Maggie thought. Aishwarya was too shy to speak in a group with her husband there and Lisa was unconscious. Alys was talking a lot. More than she had during this whole disastrous evening.

Relieved that they hadn't heard her, Maggie let out the breath she'd been holding and stooped to touch the object she'd bumped into and realized it was a pallet of water bottles.

Thank you, God, she thought as she wrestled two bottles loose from the plastic package and tucked them under her arm.

Aspirin and water. It wasn't great but it would have to do.

Silently, she slipped back through the wine cellar door, moving the footstool out of the way and easing the door silently closed behind her. With her arms full of the water bottles, she moved gingerly down the stairs.

"Grace?" she called. "I'm back, sweetie."

Maggie found her way back to Grace and immediately spread the pills out on the drape covering Grace.

"Wake up now," Maggie said, giving Grace's leg a shake.

Grace didn't move.

Maggie felt for Grace's face with her hands and gently slapped her.

"Grace! Wake up!" Maggie cried, her voice laced with the terror she felt. "Wake up! Wake up!"

"Ow! Stop it!" Grace said, feebly brushing Maggie's hands away with her good arm. "I'm awake."

"I brought you water. Here, sit up."

Maggie held the bottle to Grace's lips and Grace drank thirstily. When she stopped, Grace's body went limp with relief.

"Thank you," Grace murmured.

"I have aspirin for you to take," Maggie said.

"No aspirin," Grace said. "Anti...clotting."

"I don't know what it is," Maggie said. "It's probably not aspirin but take it anyway."

Grace gave a weak laugh. "Silly Maggie."

"I love you, Grace," Maggie said, her voice full of tears. "You are my dearest, best friend in the world and I have missed you so much."

"Me too, darling," Grace said.

"Who did this to you?"

"Not going. To believe it."

"I'll believe anything at this point. Who attacked you?"

"It was Alys."

34

ASHES TO ASHES

G race closed her eyes, her head lolling back against her
shoulder. "Sleep now," she murmured.

Maggie's mouth fell open and she stared at Grace,
her brain unable to accept what she'd just heard.

"Grace, are you sure?" Maggie asked leaning closer to Grace
and feeling the tension build in her body.

"I smelled her perfume," Grace murmured. "Alys wears *Joy*.
Very distinctive."

Maggie sat back on her heels and realized that even she
remembered noting Alys's perfume at one point. It was an old-
fashioned scent, very floral. And Grace was right. Very distinctive.

So it's Alys? she thought as her mind worked to wrap around
the idea. *Alys working with Max probably. That made sense.* Max
hated LeFleur and...well, Maggie would just have to assume that
Alys's motive for killing Manon would become clear once she was
sitting in a police interrogation room.

Soft snores emanated from where Grace lay and Maggie
didn't have the heart not to let her sleep and find some refuge
from this nightmare.

Suddenly Maggie thought of Lisa and Aishwarya sitting back

there in the dining room unmindful of the fact that they were with a serial killer who wasn't finished killing.

You will all pay

The note made sense now too. Maggie had picked up more than a few glimmers of resentment in Alys's voice in the brief time she'd been at the resort. *Alys feels like her life is unfair and why wouldn't she? surrounded by entitled people with enough money for ski holidays.*

Maggie knew she had to do something. She couldn't just wait here to be rescued, not with a serial killer among them—a serial killer who was now identified. Grace was still asleep, but Maggie felt her trembling under the cotton drapes. The drapes weren't enough to keep Grace warm. She was in shock. Maggie rubbed her hands against her cashmere sweater that she'd worn under her cardigan.

Well, that settles it, she thought grimly, her heart sinking but knowing what she must do.

Grace needs more warmth than a bunch of dusty curtains can afford.

And I cannot let Alys kill any more innocent people.

Maggie picked her way carefully through the ruined kitchen, careful not to make too much noise but not to trip either. By the time she was at the swinging door, she was sweating and her heart was pounding in her chest.

She didn't have a plan yet for what she was going to do.

She pushed open the swinging door and entered the dining room. She could see Lisa lying on the carpet with a stack of table-cloths under her head. The Patels still sat apart from each other and Serge was next to Lisa, his hands in his lap, his chin on his chest as if napping.

Only Alys was standing. She was the first one to see Maggie.

"*Oh, mon Dieu!*" Alys said. "I cannot believe you are alive!"

Yeah, I'll bet that's a big surprise, Maggie thought.

"Where have you been?" Alys asked.

"I found Grace," Maggie said as she joined them.

"You have?" Serge said, getting to his feet.

"Thank God!" Aishwarya said, her hand to her heart.

"She's hurt," Maggie said, her eyes on Alys.

"But alive?" Alys said, her face wreathed in smiles. "That is good news."

"I don't believe any of this," Raj said, frowning. "She's lying to us."

"What possible purpose would she have for lying?" Serge said to him in anger.

"Someone—one of you—came behind me and locked me into a heat conduit," Maggie said, her eyes on Alys.

Serge snorted. "That is absurd." He looked around the room as if expecting others to join in. "She is joking."

"Who else left this room besides me?" Maggie asked.

"No one left," Alys said. "You are just upsetting everyone."

"Nobody left this room?"

"Nobody but you," Raj said.

They were either protecting Alys or hadn't noticed when she'd left, Maggie thought in frustration. But now that she'd let the cat out of the bag *Alys* knew that Maggie knew it was she who attacked Grace. And yet Alys's face was calm.

Could Grace have been wrong? She did take a very nasty hit to the head.

"I need blankets," Maggie said to Alys.

"All we have are the tablecloths," Alys said. "As you know."

"No, Madame Chaix," Aishwarya said softly. "Remember? Monsieur Toureille found a stack of wool lap throws in the table linens cupboard." Aishwarya pulled one off her knees and held it out to Maggie.

"Thank you, Aishwarya," Maggie said. "I'm afraid I can't move

Grace and she's in shock. I need all the blankets you can spare."
She turned to the others. "Leave enough for Lisa."

"Of course," Alys said, gathering up the few scattered wool
throws in her arms. "Tell me where Madame Van Sant is and I
will take them to her."

Oh, you'd like that, wouldn't you?

"Not necessary," Maggie said holding her hand out for the
blankets. "I'll take them."

"I think not, Madame," Serge said, standing between Alys and
Maggie. "It is *très difficile* to trust during this time, *non?* You said
yourself we should all stay together. Besides, we only have your
word that your friend is alive. You will tell Madame Chaix where
your friend is."

Was Serge in on it with Alys?

"Not going to happen," Maggie said firmly, as Raj and Alys
joined Serge in a line facing her.

"Then your friend will be very cold," Raj said flatly.

"Would...would you allow me to go to your friend instead of
Madame Chaix?" Aishwarya asked, standing up uncertainly.

"Be quiet, Aishwarya," Raj snarled.

"Yes," Maggie said. "Yes, I would happily allow you to take the
blankets to Grace and thank you, Aishwarya." She watched as
Alys went to pile the wool blankets into Aishwarya's outstretched
arms.

"She'll need a flashlight," Maggie said.

Serge handed Aishwarya a flashlight and she nodded her
thanks to him.

"I don't know why you are doing this," Raj said in irritation to
his wife.

"Are you worried about my safety, Raj?" Aishwarya said softly.

Raj snorted and turned away. "You're just desperate for attention. It's sickening."

Aishwarya turned to where Maggie.

"Where am I going with these, Madame?" Aishwarya asked, the blankets clutched to her chest.

"It's right through the kitchen," Maggie said, moving toward Aishwarya as if to give her directions. As soon as she reached the woman, Maggie grabbed Aishwarya by the hair and stuck the steak knife that she had been working out of her pocket to the young woman's neck.

Aishwarya shrieked but didn't drop the blankets.

"What are you going?" Alys screamed. "Somebody stop her!"

"Try it," Maggie said, breathing harshly, "and I'll kill her."

35

BAD CALL

"Follow us and I swear I'll kill her," Maggie said as she began to back up with Aishwarya toward the kitchen.

"The rest of you should know that when I found Grace," Maggie said, "she told me that Alys Chaix was the one who attacked her so you can do with that information what you will."

Aishwarya stumbled and Maggie tightened her grip on her. She could feel Aishwarya trembling in her arms.

"Are you mad?" Alys said shrilly. "I am not the killer!"

"Please don't hurt me, Madame," Aishwarya whimpered.

Maggie felt a sliver of shame for what she was doing to the poor woman but it couldn't be helped.

I'm no better than her husband, Maggie thought. *I'm using her timid nature for my own means.*

When Maggie and Aishwarya reached the swinging doors, Maggie turned to Serge.

"Monsieur Toureille, I would protect Lisa if I were you since she can't protect herself. I didn't mention it earlier but I found a note left by the killer saying she wasn't done. When we are finally rescued, that note combined with our testimony will help indict Madame Chaix for these murders."

"You are mad," Alys said as she shook her head.

"If you're smart you'll tie Alys up," Maggie said. "Otherwise I'd keep my distance and not get close enough for her to sink a steak knife into your ribs while you wait for rescue."

"You mean like *you* are threatening to do with my wife?" Raj shouted.

Maggie knew Raj could care less what happened to his wife.

All the same, his words hit home. Hard.

Maggie wasn't surprised to see that no one in the dining room group made a move to stop her or follow them. She probably looked unhinged to them. Nor did anyone want to be in the kitchen which was now dropping pieces of its ceiling every few minutes.

But Grace was through that kitchen and, falling ceiling or not, that's where she and Aishwarya were going.

The minute they were in the kitchen she released Aishwarya.

"I'm sorry about that," Maggie said, pulling the blankets from Aishwarya's arms. "You can go back to the others now. Just don't turn your back on Alys."

"Where is your friend?" Aishwarya said, looking around the kitchen. The center of the space was obliterated by a huge section of the ceiling and plaster continued to shake down in various spots overhead as if there was a disco on the floor above them. "Do you need help?"

"I could use some," Maggie admitted. "She's back here in the wine cellar."

Using the flashlight, she turned and gingerly picked her way back to the door of the cellar. Aishwarya followed closely. Maggie opened the door to the wine cellar and positioned the footstool to hold it open. She could see that nearly half the ceiling had come down while Maggie was gone.

With a frantic cry, Maggie ran down the stairs.

"Grace! Grace!"

She ran to where she'd left Grace and saw that chunks of the ceiling beams had fallen and narrowly missed Grace. Grace was lying underneath two beams that formed a crude cross over her.

Oh, thank God, Maggie thought as she shone the flashlight on Grace's face and saw that she was still breathing.

Aishwarya stood at the top of the stairs.

"We have to move her," Maggie said. "I'll slip the blanket under her and create a sling." She shined the light on the stairs so that Aishwarya could see as she edged down to where Maggie and Grace were. Between the two of them they got Grace into the sling and each took one end of the blanket.

"It's freezing down here," Aishwarya said. "Much colder even than the kitchen."

"All the more reason to get her out," Maggie said, eyeing the ceiling again. An ominous cracking sound shook down a heavy scattering of plaster and dust across their shoulders.

Next time it would be stone and wood.

"Hurry," Maggie urged, her voice hoarse.

They half dragged, half carried Grace in the blanket to the steps and then painfully moved her up the stairs one agonizing step at a time until they reached the threshold of the kitchen.

"Careful. There's water on the floor," Maggie said. "Help me get her on that bench next to the sinks."

They struggled to drag Grace to the bench and then on the count of three managed to swing her up onto it, a good foot off the ground.

Maggie and Aishwarya were both sweating when Maggie began to pile the other blankets on top of Grace.

Aishwarya knelt by Grace and smoothed away the damp golden curls from Grace's face.

"She is so beautiful," Aishwarya said. "Her husband must be worried about her."

"She doesn't have a husband," Maggie said, leaning against the prep counter as she tried to get her heart rate back down to normal levels. "But she has plenty of people who would be very upset if anything happened to her."

Me, for one, Maggie thought.

Grace fluttered her eyes open as Aishwarya withdrew her hand.

"Alys..." Grace murmured.

"No, darling," Maggie said. "It's Aishwarya. She's helping us."

Grace frowned, her eyes squeezed shut and she shook her head. "No," she said. "Ow."

"Stop shaking your head. You probably have a concussion."

"Alys," Grace said again.

Dear God, was Grace brain damaged? Maggie thought her eyes blinking rapidly with worry as she watched her friend.

Grace was quiet again and Maggie watched the gentle rise and fall of her chest as she succumbed once more to sleep.

"Is she badly hurt do you think?" Aishwarya asked as she stood by the counter and rubbed the chill off her arms. A chunk of plaster the size of a toaster fell not two feet from where they stood. Aishwarya glanced up at the ceiling.

Later Maggie would say it was this moment—the moment when Aishwarya glanced up at the ceiling as if it were nothing more than an annoying leaky pipe and not a thousand tons of plaster and wooden beam and snow about to pummel them— that made her realize the truth.

Aishwarya's reaction was not the reaction of a normal person.

And when Maggie realized Aishwarya didn't look anywhere near as petrified as Maggie herself felt it made her remember something that had literally been in her face since she grabbed Aishwarya and held her close when they walked out of the dining room together.

It was something that Maggie had registered on some level but ignored. She'd been so worried about getting back to Grace and not being attacked by the dining room that she completely missed the fact that Aishwarya's perfume was familiar.

When Maggie finally stopped thinking about how afraid she was to die in this room and never see Laurent or Jemmy and Mila again, she realized what she should have known the minute Grace kept insisting the killer was Alys.

Grace hadn't seen her attacker.

Grace only knew it was Alys by her scent. Alys wore *Joy*. Grace's attacker wore *Joy*.

"That's a lovely perfume you're wearing," Maggie said to Aishwarya.

Instantly, Aishwarya's face altered, the innocent sweetness dissolved away.

"Thank you," she said, narrowing her eyes as she tried to interpret Maggie's compliment.

"It's *Joy*, isn't it? I recognize it because it's one of my mother's favorites."

Aishwarya's gaze held Maggie's, her lips pressed together in a firm line.

"Or maybe it was my grandmother's," Maggie said. "It's so old-fashioned. Which is odd because I think Alys wears it too."

"Does she?"

"In fact, it's how I know it was you who attacked Grace," Maggie said bluntly.

The emotions that passed across Aishwarya's face told Maggie that the woman was trying to decide whether to come clean or continue to lie.

She must have decided there was no more reason to lie.

"You're an idiot," Aishwarya said, her lips pulled back in scorn. "Blaming poor moronic Alys. The stupid cow can barely tie her own apron. You ought to be ashamed."

"I guess I *am* an idiot," Maggie admitted, watching the woman carefully.

She couldn't help but notice that now that they were in the kitchen they were literally surrounded by knives.

"Do you mind telling me why?" Maggie said. "Why the chef? Why Grace? None of it makes any sense to me."

"And none of it will make any sense to the police either."

"I assume you think I won't be around to enlighten them."

"That is correct," Aishwarya said, her white teeth flashing in the dim light. "But I'm happy to tell you since you won't live to tell anyone else."

Maggie still had the steak knife in her pocket. *Aishwarya must know I do.* It was worrisome that knowing she did didn't seem to upset Aishwarya.

Maggie positioned herself between Aishwarya and where Grace lay on the bench.

"Let me guess," Maggie said, hoping to distract her and stretch this out for as long as she could. "You went to the kitchen to poison someone's dish and the chef saw you."

"Bingo, as you Yanks say." Aishwarya grinned and took a step closer to Maggie, one hand resting lightly on the nearest prep counter. "Keep going. I'd love to see how much you've guessed."

"Well, I'd say when you stormed out of the dining room the first time, you had enough time to go into the kitchen via the access by the men's room and stick a knife in Monsieur LeFleur since he certainly wasn't expecting it."

Aishwarya smiled.

"But somehow the poisoned dish found its way to Detective Thompson. I assume he was collateral damage?"

Aishwarya shrugged, her eyes glittering with pleasure as she watched Maggie.

"Then when the avalanche hit and everything went to hell that must have thrown you."

"Not really. I just became more flexible."

"Why did you attack Grace? Did she see you kill Manon?"

"I'd already taken care of Madame Toureille when your friend came upon us in the hallway."

"You mean, as you were attempting to position the mannequin in the fish tank?"

"It was dark so I knew she hadn't seen my face but it was easier just to bash her on the head than try to come up with an excuse for what I was doing. Besides, Manon's body was on the floor. It was a miracle your friend didn't trip over it."

"So you hit Grace on the head with your flashlight and dragged her to the heating grate."

"I'd planned on putting Manon in there so I already had the cover off. With the amount of blood gushing out of your friend's head I knew she'd bleed to death soon enough. I pushed her in and since the conduit was at an incline she slid to the end. Rather like a garbage chute!"

Maggie bit back her fury at hearing how Grace had been attacked and left for dead.

"Then once she was inside, I shoved Manon's body in behind her and finished decorating the fish tank."

"Why go to all the bother?"

"Are you serious? I wanted you to think the killer was Manon, of course. And you did, didn't you?"

"And then after killing two women you came back to the dining room and played the victim. So is your husband in on this? Or was it *his* plate you were trying to poison in the kitchen that the unlucky Detective Thompson got a hold of?"

"Raj? Seriously? You mean you don't know?" Aishwarya cocked her head to look at Maggie with a quizzical look.

"Don't know what?" Maggie said with exasperation.

"It was you, of course," Aishwarya said.

"Me?" Maggie said, dumbfounded.

"Huh. I guess you really don't know. I think it's because so many American television shows make us all believe that the

Yanks are so clever when it comes to solving mysteries and so on. But you're really not that smart at all."

"Why did you want to kill *me*? I don't even know you."

"Of course you don't," Aishwarya said, taking another step forward. "But it became clear to me that *getting to know you* was precisely what my husband was keen to do. Oh, and by the way, thanks so much for *protecting* me from my own husband."

"You're out of your mind," Maggie said in bewilderment. "I never exchanged two words with your husband."

"That's a lie. From the moment you showed up Raj hasn't been able to take his eyes off you."

"You're demented. I'm a forty year old woman with two kids."

"I'm as astonished as you are, believe me. One thing I learned a very long time ago however is that there's no accounting for taste."

"How did you lock me in the hall conduit?"

"It wasn't difficult. It was dark. As soon as you left, I slipped away. Thanks for separating me from Raj by the way. I knew you were trying to get him to yourself but it at least served the purpose of allowing me to slip away unobserved. Anyway, I followed you and saw you go down the transit. Honestly, I couldn't believe my luck! I still had the screws in my pocket and a steak knife. I had the cover back on and tightened before you even knew I was there."

"You're telling me nobody saw you leave?" Maggie said. "You must have walked right past Raj to get here."

"He didn't see me."

"No," Maggie said. "He saw you and didn't care."

"It doesn't matter what he saw or didn't see," Aishwarya said angrily through gritted teeth. "Raj and I have a long life together ahead of us. I'll make him care."

"Boy, that sounds fun. And now?" Maggie asked.

"You tell me. You're the one with the steak knife."

So she hadn't forgotten about it. Again, Maggie felt a fissure of misgiving wondering what the woman knew that made her so confident.

"Well," Maggie said, "my plan is that we wait until we're rescued and then you go to prison until you're an old woman."

Aishwarya's teeth bared again. "Or, how about I kill you and your friend and tell the authorities I fought you and barely escaped with my life?"

"How is that going to work since *I'm* the one holding the knife?"

"By the time you get up the courage to defend yourself, you'll be bleeding out."

"I wouldn't count on that. I'm feeling pretty murderous about now."

"Typical American. Full of bluster. And oh, did I mention, I also have this?"

Aishwarya took another step closer and held up the chef's knife in her hand, the sleeve of her wool cardigan falling away to reveal a muscular arm.

"And unlike you I won't hesitate to use it," Aishwarya said as she lunged across the short distance that separated them.

36

OUT OF TIME

As she saw Aishwarya rush to close the distance between them, the large knife flashing before her, Maggie dropped the flashlight and spun away, desperately fumbling for her small kitchen knife.

Even without the light, Aishwarya had anticipated Maggie's move. Maggie felt the stomach-lurching suddenness as Aishwarya's blade slashed across her shoulder as she tried to twist out of reach.

The pain in her arm lit up the room in a searing white hot spasm of agony. Maggie faltered, falling to her knees, the pain in her shoulder leaving her breathless.

She was aware of a dullness creeping into her brain as she pulled her knife free from her pocket as if in slow motion. Her knees were drenched from the water on the floor.

"I saw you looking at him!" Aishwarya hissed, rushing Maggie again, the sharp blade singing through the air.

Maggie didn't have time to get to her feet. She flipped onto her back and kicked hard against the slashing arm as Aishwarya loomed over her, the knife coming down hard.

Her foot connected with Aishwarya's arm. Aishwarya grunted

as Maggie's kick knocked her arm. But she still had the knife. Maggie was wedged up against something heavy behind her where she could go no further. For one indecisive moment, she hesitated before turning to slip under the prep table.

But not before Aishwarya's knife found her.

The blade sliced across Maggie's back, peeling back her sweater and a thin stripe of bare flesh beneath.

Maggie tensed her body at the onslaught of pain, her hand still tightly gripping the steak knife.

"As soon as you come out it's shish kabob time," Aishwarya shouted.

Maggie rolled to the other side of the prep table and pulled herself to her feet. Without the flashlight it was hard to see more than just a dark shape moving.

But that dark shape was moving toward where Grace lay.

"It occurs to me that I know of a way to get you to show yourself," Aishwarya said.

"Stop!" Maggie said. "Leave her alone."

Aishwarya turned to face Maggie. "Happy to. All you have to do is toss down your knife and walk into this one. Think you can manage that?"

Maggie hoisted herself onto the prep table and swung her legs over the edge closest to Aishwarya.

"Fine," she said. "You win." The pain in her shoulder should have been vying with the one across her back but oddly, Maggie felt no pain, only numbness.

"Throw down the knife," Aishwarya said.

This was the moment, Maggie knew. The moment that would determine if she ever saw Laurent again, if she ever held her children again, if Grace ever got her second chance.

This moment. This terrible unendurable moment.

Three pieces of ceiling fell in quick succession around Maggie. A loud creaking splintered the wall holding the bank of sinks, still accordioned under the half-caved ceiling. They groaned and leaned close to the floor.

"Any time now," Aishwarya said.

Suddenly a strip of industrial pendant lights hanging over the prep table sputtered on and then went back out again. Maggie was able to see Aishwarya's face as she glanced in surprise at the lights.

"Do it now!" Aishwarya said harshly, twisting around to hold the butcher knife over Grace's inert body.

Maggie held her small knife away from her body and then dropped it. At the same time she heard a loud hum as the refrigerator turned on. The lights flickered on again and stayed on this time.

"The back-up generators must have finally kicked in," Maggie said.

Seeing the kitchen with the lights on brought a convulsion of horror through Maggie. She could see the damage now. She could see Grace lying lifelessly on the bench, her hand hung limply over the edge. She could see the madness in Aishwarya's face as she advanced on Maggie, her eyes glittering with intent, her feet sloshing through the ankle-deep water.

"Drop that knife or I kill her! I mean it!" Aishwarya shrieked.

"I already dropped it," Maggie said holding up her empty hands. "See? It's gone."

Aishwarya looked around to confirm that there was nothing on the counter next to Maggie except a stand mixer and a scattering of wooden spoons. A look of triumph spread on her face.

Maggie waited. It took every ounce of willpower she had to do it. She watched Aishwarya come closer and closer, the knife held out at chest level and never wavering. Then without taking her eyes off Aishwarya's face Maggie felt for the *on* button on the commercial mixer on the table next to her. The sound of its engine was almost as overpowering as the sound of the blood pounding in Maggie's ears.

And she pushed it off the counter onto the floor.

Instantly, a lightning jolt sparked and Aishwarya convulsed in a seizure before falling into the shallow water, her knife clattering to the tabletop. Aishwarya fell face first into the flooded kitchen floor.

The splashing continued as Maggie realized that Aishwarya was flailing involuntarily as her heart went into ventricular fibrillation.

Maggie sat on the counter, her hands clapped to her mouth, her eyes squeezed shut. The silence in the room was interrupted only by the sounds of dripping and the still-running mixer in the water. Maggie cradled her injured arm against her chest, her blood thrumming in her ears, her gaze finally directed but unseeing on the dead body in the ankle deep water beneath her.

Horror and shame coursed through Maggie as she stared at Aishwarya's still twitching body face down in the shallow water in front of the stove. The hum of the electric mixer seemed to get louder and louder in Maggie's ears.

With the pain in her shoulder making her dizzy, Maggie fought a creeping confusion as she got on her knees and crawled to the end of the prep table. Carefully, she shifted her weight to the kitchen counter against the wall. She didn't see any water on the floor here and eased down gently to stand on a spot next to the bench where Grace lay.

She put her hand on Grace's forehead. "Please don't die, Grace. Zouzou needs you. I need you."

Grace's eyes opened and then closed again. "Are we...back in business?" she asked softly.

Maggie knelt beside her and kissed her cheek. "Yes, dearest. We are."

"Well. All right then," Grace said as she slowly lost her battle to stay conscious.

37

WISHING ON THE MOON

Maggie eased herself to a sitting position on the bench next to Grace and with shaking hands gently pulled Grace's head on her lap. She knew she should try to bind the cut on her throbbing shoulder but the prospect was too much for her.

She listened to the hum and whirl of the mixer in the water. Her eyes grew hot at the sound and she desperately wished she'd thought to turn it off.

The sound was nearly unnatural; a relentless low-grade hum muffled by being underwater and a constant admonition of what she'd just done.

I've killed a person. A young person who'd been alive just five minutes earlier.

Maggie ran a hand over her face. She closed her eyes, praying for sleep, for unconsciousness, in the bright humming kitchen full of water and blood and death.

She thought she heard a dog barking.

"*Allo*, anyone!" The voice sounding like it came from very far away.

Maggie opened her eyes and saw a figure descending into the

room from the ceiling. He was wearing a bright orange vest with a climbing harness. He wore a mask so that at first, Maggie thought she was looking at some kind of alien being.

She watched with stunned curiosity as he lowered himself on a rope into the center of the kitchen. Suddenly a shiver of premonition jolted her up out of her detachment.

"Wait!" Maggie screamed. She stood and waved with her uninjured arm. Instantly her legs buckled and she fell back to a sitting position onto the bench.

"There's water on the floor here," she called, "and a live wire or something." She gripped the edge of the counter and watched the man as he dropped lightly onto one of the tabletops.

He gave her a thumbs up sign to indicate that he understood and then walked across the counter, knocking bowls and wooden spoons into the water below. He hesitated only briefly as he passed LeFleur's body.

"You are hurt, Madame?" he said as he knelt on the prep table and unplugged the mixer. Instantly the whirling hum ceased.

Aishwarya's body was in plain view on the floor before him.

"It's my friend," Maggie said. "She has a head injury."

The man eased himself off the counter into the shallow water. He came to her and knelt beside her, his hands going to her shoulder. Maggie was shocked to realize that the front of her sweater was crimson with her blood.

Behind him, Maggie saw another man appear from the dining room entrance.

Maggie shook her head with disbelief as she watched her rescuer quickly examine Grace and begin to prepare an IV for her on the spot.

"What took you guys so long?"

"The road to the inn was blocked," he said grimly, checking Grace's vital signs before turning to Maggie, his eyes on her shoulder. "We couldn't get through and the weather was too bad to use air support until an hour ago."

"There's...there's no ambulance outside?" Maggie felt the relief she'd felt from the rescue begin to wane. Fear crept up and clutched her throat.

He pulled the sleeve of Maggie sweater down and shook his head when he saw the wound. Quickly, he pulled a bandage from his backpack and expertly bound Maggie's shoulder. As he worked, more plaster from the ceiling rained down.

"You are not to worry, Madame," the man said firmly. "You are rescued."

Maggie wanted to laugh at his hubris. But she also wanted to kiss him because now the responsibility for keeping them alive was his, not hers.

"We'll need the stretcher," he said and it was a moment before Maggie realized he was not talking to her. Two men appeared behind him.

"Where are the others?" Maggie asked. "They were in the dining room."

"Your friends are already out of the chalet and being treated."

A large piece of ceiling fell, splashing into the shallow water, followed by the ominous creaking of one of the larger supporting beams. The rescuer looked up.

"Can you walk, Madame?" he asked.

"Yes," Maggie said as she watched two men return with a folding stretcher. She edged out of their way as they tucked Grace into a thermal cover and slid her onto the stretcher.

They turned to eye Maggie as if unsure of her ability to walk out on her own.

"You will follow us closely, *oui*, Madame?"

Maggie nodded and then felt a wave of dizziness crash into her. She reached for the counter to steady herself but used the wrong arm. The blistering inferno of pain that ricocheted through her shoulder made her stumble.

"Pierre!" one of the men shouted. "*Venez immediatement!*"

As she sank to her knees Maggie felt the water drench her

pant legs. It occurred to her that she must have walked away from the one dry spot in the kitchen. She wanted to put her head down, even in the water. Just for a moment. Just to rest.

Suddenly she felt herself being pulled upward. Before she could try to stand strong arms pulled her off her feet and lifted her close to a massive chest.

Maggie tried to open her eyes but nausea hit her when she did. She squeezed her eyes shut.

The sound of the ceiling beginning to fall was a succession of what sounded like deafening shot gun blasts reverberating throughout the kitchen, flinging plaster and wood in erratic patterns around the room. An unholy elongated creaking sound, so loud it blotted out everything else, seemed to herald the impending final fall of the kitchen ceiling.

In spite of that the man who carried her walked slowly. Maggie heard the sounds of his boots splashing in the water as he edged furniture and debris out of his way. Every time she lifted her head to try to see, the nausea returned.

The man whose arms she was in leaned down at one point and spoke softly, his breath lightly tinged by the scent of wine.

"Are you the wife of the big guy who tried to climb down here with me and my men?" he said almost jovially.

Laurent!

Maggie felt a surge of euphoria. She nodded in spite of the dizziness and her eyes stung with tears.

"Yes," she said, swallowing past a lump in her throat. "Yes, he's mine."

And even though she wasn't out of the demolished chalet and the ceiling was raining down all around her, and even though she was so cold she couldn't move her fingers, when Maggie realized Laurent was near, she closed her eyes and finally relaxed.

Her rescuer carried her through a narrow opening of the debris and broken furniture that the rescuers had created with their axes between the dining room and the lobby. The front window that had showcased the lobby by the registration desk was gone, replaced by an ominous black barricade of snow, broken lobby furniture and trees.

Before Maggie could wonder how they were going to get out of the building, her rescuer turned and headed for the stairs leading to the upstairs bedrooms. Although the front of the chalet was demolished, amazingly, the inside stairs—although creaking loudly as the man ran up them—had been virtually untouched by the avalanche.

The man carrying her turned into the first bedroom off the stairs and ran to the window facing the front of the chalet. The cold slammed into Maggie as soon as he put her on her feet in front of the window. She was astonished to realize it was daylight outside. The snow sloped past the front drive where a single bright red helicopter sat, its rotors moving continuously, its exhaust creating dark clouds in the grey light.

Beyond the air ambulance a small tent was set up at the foot of the steep mound of snow that connected the upstairs bedroom window to the ground by way of the chalet's starkly slanting roofline. Maggie squinted into the light and saw several figures below. She thought she recognized Alys draped in a heavy thermal blanket standing by the helicopter.

"Maggie!"

Maggie strained to see him. She lurched forward to climb out the window, tears already streaming down her cheek and instantly freezing in the frigid air.

"Laurent!" she croaked but not loud enough for anyone to hear.

"*Un moment, Madame,*" her rescuer said sternly as he grabbed her by her arm. He pulled on a rope and hauled a battered rescue sled through the window. "I will deliver you to your husband after we alight from the roof, yes?"

Suddenly Maggie felt the floor beneath her begin to shimmy. She grabbed for the window frame but it was moving too as the room started to break up. The overhead ceiling lamp crashed to the carpeted floor and the tall dresser tipped over as the floor buckled and gave way.

Her rescuer grabbed Maggie and threw her face down onto the sled perched on the rim before flinging himself on top of her as the window began to break apart. His breath coming in panicked pants in Maggie's ear he pushed them off the window sill of the quickly disintegrating building.

Maggie closed her eyes and felt the world swirl around her in a nauseating vortex, her breath gone from the pressure of the man on top of her and the sudden cold as the sled burst free of the chalet and careened down the steep embankment to the bottom below.

She felt the sled hit level ground and the man rolled off her into the snow. Gasping, she squinted against the bright light of the day but didn't have the strength to do more than lift her head. The world began to shift again and she closed her eyes against the onslaught of cold and light.

And then she felt Laurent's arms around her.

She tried to wrap her arms around his neck but she couldn't lift them.

"I'm okay," she said breathlessly, more for herself than for Laurent. Her eyes wide and glowing as he held her close. She wanted to ask where Grace was. She wanted to tell him how much she loved him and how glad she was to be alive. But all she could do was tremble with the sheer pleasure of having his arms around her, even the feel of the biting wind against her face.

Laurent kissed her face and scooped her up into his arms before striding to the waiting helicopter.

It would be the last thing Maggie remembered that day.

38

ONE WEEK LATER

Maggie walked into the kitchen at Domaine St-Buvard where Laurent stood with his hands on his hips as Zouzou sprinkled spices onto the raw pork chops.

"Smells good," Maggie said cheerfully.

"Nothing is cooking yet," Laurent said as he turned and handed Maggie two glasses of wine and nodded at the French doors that led to the terrace.

"I'm going, I'm going," Maggie said good-naturedly. It had only been a week since the rescue but Laurent still refused to allow her to do much in the way of anything around the house. Maggie very much feared she was going to get way too comfortable being waited on hand and foot.

"Dinner in one hour," Laurent called after her.

"I'll try not to leave town before then," Maggie said as she walked toward Grace who was waiting for her by the French doors.

Grace was holding two wool throws and took one of the wine glasses from Maggie.

"I heard," she said with a smile. "We have an hour."

Maggie glanced into the living room where Mia, Jemmy and

her father were playing a board game in front of the fireplace. Elspeth sat on the couch watching them. Maggie couldn't help notice that her mother looked older and even more fretful than the last time she'd seen her.

My dad's condition is getting to her, she thought as she moved out the door that Grace held open. Instantly a cold breeze rearranged her hair and she shivered and hurried to the two lounge chairs that Laurent had set up next to one of the tall outdoor heaters.

Wordlessly, she and Grace settled down onto the loungers and arranged the throws across their knees. The light had left the sky hours earlier but there was still visible the ghostly specter of the vineyard under a nearly full moon.

She turned to Grace and lifted her glass in a toast.

"You'll miss these endless nightly drink-a-thons out on our back terrace," she said with a mischievous grin.

Grace laughed and took a sip of her wine. "It's been heaven," she agreed.

"After going through sheer hell first," Maggie reminded her.

"Isn't that always the way?"

The past week had been a pleasant one, punctuated by visits to the doctor for their various breaks and scrapes as well as interviews with the police and insurance agents for the ski property. As it happened the planned week to find their way back to each other that they'd hoped to have in the mountains had happened once they'd succeeded in surviving the experience.

They'd spent the last week in slow walks through the vineyard and in long evenings enjoying wine and shared confidences. It was amazing to Maggie that it had only been a week since they'd been rescued from the demolished chalet outside Grenoble. And now it was time for Grace to leave and go back to her life in Atlanta.

"What will you do when you get back?" Maggie asked. Grace and Zouzou's flight was tomorrow afternoon out of Marseille.

Grace rearranged the cashmere shawl draping her sling. "I talked to Windsor last night. He and Susie want to adopt Taylor's baby."

"Really?"

"It's probably a good idea. I don't know. I'm just not sure what I think about it."

"Anything else?"

Grace shrugged and then immediately winced. "I got an email from my job at the library. They don't need me anymore."

"Oh, Grace..."

"It's just as well. It was only part-time. It made me think I was doing something but really it was no money. If not for Windsor's child support Zouzou and I would be eating catsup packets."

"You're always welcome here."

Grace smiled at her, her eyes glistening with emotion. "Thank you, darling. But I'm not sure what in the world I'd do. I'm not a writer like you and I don't really have any skills or talents."

"That's not true," Maggie said softly but it did occur to her that the sorts of things that Grace was good at—dressing well, being witty and beautiful to look at—were not things that necessarily paid very well.

They sipped in silence for a moment and Maggie couldn't help but note that there was no tension or uncomfortable silence between them.

Just like in the old days, she thought.

"How's your shoulder?" Grace asked.

Maggie wore a matching sling to cradle her wounded arm.

"Fine. And yours?"

Grace laughed. "This detective work really does bang us up pretty good, doesn't it?"

"That's for sure. Remember the last time we both had matching slings? Our first case together when we found out who murdered Connor?"

The words were out of Maggie's mouth before she thought

and she instantly gave Grace a worried look. As Zouzou's biological father, Connor had caused nearly as many problems dead as he had alive. But still, Grace had been fond of him.

Grace smiled. "I remember."

"I still can't believe it was just a week ago," Maggie said.

"Alys called me this afternoon," Grace said. "She said she was too embarrassed to call you herself but she wanted me to pass on her apologies for thinking you were a brutal serial killer."

"Aw, that's sweet. But then I kind of did the same thing to her."

"She found a job in an accounting firm in Lyons. As I understand it, it's closer to a better doctor for her son, too."

"Oh, that's wonderful! Plus it'll probably mean less weird hours for her so she can be with him more," Maggie said. "Any news on what happened to the others?"

The last glimpse she'd had of Raj was in the medic tent in front of the chalet where they'd all huddled until another emergency helicopter transport could take them to the Grenoble hospital.

Raj had been sitting on a camp cot, a forgotten mug of tea in both hands, staring at the five bodies that had been brought out of the inn. Maggie would have given a lot to have spoken to him to see how he was processing it all and how he was registering the fact of being so completely wrong about his wife. Plus she was curious if what he now knew meant he'd changed in any way.

From the little that Maggie had known Raj, she doubted it.

"Alys said Lisa was still in the hospital but expected to fully recover. Serge left her to go to his children. I take it they're relatively young and with their mother now gone..."

"It's terrible. But so Serge just left Lisa?"

"He did. But here's something interesting. It seems Serge had spoken with the chef before dinner earlier that night to get him to embed an *engagement ring* in Lisa's custard and then serve it to her."

"You're kidding. He was going to propose? But he was already married to Manon."

"It's possible it was the gesture more than anything," Grace said.

"It might explain why he seemed so worried about me going in and out of the kitchen," Maggie thought, frowning. "I thought it was because he knew I'd find LeFleur's body." She looked at Grace. "So I take it he decided against proposing to her?"

"Pretty sure the moment for that was spoiled right around the time Lisa accused him of killing Manon."

"That would do it."

Through the French doors, Maggie glimpsed Laurent standing in the door of the kitchen talking with Zouzou. He'd performed some kind of miracle on the child while Grace and Maggie were gone. Nobody was surprised of course. After all, it was Laurent.

"So tell me again why you left the dining room in the middle of the night?" Maggie asked. "I was sure you were going to do some Nancy Drew ninja moves to get back in my good graces or something. I was totally wracked with guilt."

Grace laughed. "I *was* pretty desperate to get back in your good graces I'll admit. And you were right. I saw someone slip away so I went to check it out."

"That was brave."

Grace smiled at the unspoken words between them: *And also crazy.*

"You couldn't tell it was Aishwarya?"

"It was so dark I could barely see my hands in front of my face."

"Next time bring a flashlight."

"Thank you, darling."

They laughed again and Maggie felt a surge of love for her friend as she envisioned Grace tiptoeing down the darkened hallway, determined to find out who it was who had snuck out of the dining room.

"Anyway, as you know I couldn't see who it was, but I did recognize the perfume," Grace said. "I figured that out just as my foot hit something on the ground."

"Manon's body."

Grace nodded grimly. "I leaned over to see what it was and that's when everything went to black. Roll credits."

"At least you were able to identify the perfume,"

"For all the good it did me. Who could imagine that more than one person in this century would be wearing *Joy*? Let alone two women trapped in an avalanche?"

The detectives who processed the crime scene at the chalet discovered a bottle of *Joy* perfume—stolen from Alys Chaix's desk drawer—in Aishwarya Patel's purse. Clearly it was another example of Aishwarya believing Raj was attracted to someone else and needing to appropriate any tools that might be the reason for it.

Soon after they'd come home Laurent had revealed to Maggie that he'd been told that Aishwarya was recently discharged from a mental hospital, a fact that had been kept from Raj and his family in order that the arranged marriage would take place.

"In any case," Grace said, "I got hit on the head and pretty much made a mess of everything. So much for my trying to help."

"No, Grace, if you *hadn't* left in the middle of the night like you did, we wouldn't have found out who the killer was," Maggie said earnestly. "If you hadn't left, I wouldn't have gone looking for you and I wouldn't have found Manon's body. If you hadn't left, I'd have sat there in the dining room waiting for help like everyone else and I would have died because Aishwarya would eventually have found her moment to kill me. And I'd never have known it was coming."

"Well, when you put it that way...."

"Just, next time, wake me first, okay?"

"Next time?"

"Do you doubt it?"

Because of the excitement of all the travel the next day, it took longer than usual that night to get the children settled. Laurent was in already in bed reading an article on his iPad by the time Maggie climbed in next to him, mindful of her sling. Carefully navigating every day life with her injury was a constant reminder of how close she'd come to never again feeling the security and comfort of her own cozy bed with Laurent beside her.

He stretched out an arm to pull her close and she snuggled against his chest.

"What are you reading?" she asked.

"An article on building temporary housing for seasonal workers," he said.

"Really?" Maggie frowned but Laurent closed the iPad before she could see the article.

"The light, *chérie*?" Laurent said, nodding at the bedside lamp on Maggie's side of the bed.

"You're thinking of building hostels? On Domaine St-Buvard?"

"I am absolutely *not* thinking that, *non*," Laurent said. "The light?"

"Then why are you reading the article?"

"It is for a friend."

Laurent raised an eyebrow to indicate that the bedside lamp was still on but Maggie wouldn't be put off so easily.

"I need to ask you something," Maggie said.

Laurent leaned over and kissed her. "The answer is yes," he said.

She watched his eyes carefully. He'd only given her a very sketchy idea of what had happened while she and Grace were gone. But her mother had relayed the fact that she'd asked Laurent to move the family back to Atlanta.

"Yes to whatever I'm going to ask you?" Maggie asked.

"*Oui.*"

"Even if it's to sell Domaine St-Buvard and move back to Atlanta?"

"Yes, even then."

Maggie put her hand on Laurent's chest and gazed into his eyes.

"I want you to know that I'm absolutely grateful and floored that you would do something like that for me. So please don't take this the wrong way when I ask you what is happening with you and the vineyard?"

"I don't know what you mean."

"I'm not saying you wouldn't be willing to leave even if you were still in love with Domaine St-Buvard but I know that something has happened to change your feelings and before we think about making any changes at all, you need to be honest with me about what those are."

"Maggie, it is late."

"So best get talking. Morning will be here before you know it."

Laurent huffed out a sigh and then seemed to resign himself to the inevitable.

"The vineyard is not paying for itself," he said.

"It never has," she said. "But we have Aunt Delphine's money."

"*That* is the problem. We have Aunt Delphine's money."

"Okay. You know how you and I have this language gap? *That* right there what you just said. How can the inheritance be a problem?"

"Because it means the vineyard is a hobby. It is not... *necessary*. You see?'

Maggie's mouth dropped open in surprise.

"Is this why you're okay with our moving back to Atlanta? Because it lets you off the hook with keeping the vineyard?"

"I am not understanding you."

"Let me be clear then—and I'm sorry to make your life more difficult—but I have no intention of moving us back to Atlanta."

"But, *chérie*, your father—"

"I know. And you're right. It would be a lot easier for them if I were nearby."

"Elspeth would never agree to moving to France," Laurent said. "I have suggested that to her. She was adamant. All John's doctors are in Atlanta."

"I'm sure they are. But I'll bet Aix has decent doctors too for this sort of thing. I've given this some thought, Laurent. And I love you for being willing to leave but if my mother truly needs me she'll have to come to *me*. And *you* will just have to find a reason to continue working our vineyard even if it's not for the money."

Laurent's eyes glittered with excitement as he turned to face Maggie in bed. Mindful of her shoulder, he kissed her.

"Are you sure, *chérie*?"

"Positive. Now tell me what's going on. You've been acting strange all week. What's up?"

Laurent laughed and cupped Maggie's cheek with his hand.

"You know me so well. *Oui*, perhaps there is something else on my mind."

"I knew it." Maggie tipped her face toward him with curiosity and building excitement.

"But what I am going to suggest to you, *chérie*, I will need for you to be with me as a partner—even more than I did with the vineyard."

Maggie clicked off the bedroom lamp and snuggled against Laurent's chest.

"This I gotta hear," she said.

39

SIX MONTHS LATER

The shade on the terrace was deep, the sky nearly obliterated by the leafy branches of the giant plantain trees that formed a canopy over Maggie and Grace where they sat in lounge chairs on Maggie's back terrace. Tall glasses of iced coffee sat on the wrought iron table next to them as they basked in the heat of the midsummer afternoon.

Every once in awhile, they heard Zouzou's voice—high and happy—coming to them from inside the house where she stood next to Laurent in the kitchen preparing vegetables for the grill for tonight's meal.

It turned out Zouzou was passionately interested in cooking. Since she'd believed that food caused her weight problem it was a revelation to her that she might be allowed to learn to cook and not gain weight. Zouzou had lost enough weight in the last six months, Maggie noted, for her size to no longer be the first thing one saw when she entered a room.

"What are they making in there, do you know?" Grace asked.

"I think we're having chicken with rosemary and roasted veggies on the grill," Maggie said. "And a potato gratin with goat cheese."

"Mm-mm. Did I hear that Danielle and Jean-Luc are coming over for dinner?"

"They are."

Maggie turned her attention to the view of the vineyard before her. This close to harvest time, it was no surprise that it was literally crawling with workers.

"Does it unnerve you to see so many people all over Domaine St-Buvard?" Grace said.

Maggie frowned, thinking about it for a moment.

"They're not really around the house much," Maggie said. "Honestly, it makes me feel like we have our own little commune here. I actually feel safer with them here. Not that I was insecure before."

Last spring Laurent had bought Jean-Luc's vineyards and also all of Eduard Marceau's and had employed the homeless people from the Abbaye de Sainte-Trinité to work the land.

They came to the fields every day to learn the skill of cultivating grapes. Back at the Abbaye de Sainte-Trinité, Laurent had put money into modernizing the winemaking facilities in the monastery's centuries-old *cave*.

While Laurent paid the people working for him a living wage on top of helping them learn a trade, the arrangement also benefited Domaine St-Buvard in ways other than just altruistic. This would be the first year that Laurent did not have to rely on seasonal migrant workers to harvest the grapes. Or need to turn to machines for picking them. And because the families that harvested the fields had also helped plant and prune the same fields in the spring, they were more invested in helping to create a better end product.

Even Maggie could see that the expansion of the vineyard had caused a dramatic shift in Laurent's day to day affect. He joked that having twenty young people working his now two hundred and fifty plus hectare property was like having two dozen sons eager to learn everything he had to teach them.

He frequently told Maggie that as grateful as the families were—and the monastery where the single men still lived—he felt like he got much more out of the arrangement.

Maggie knew he didn't mean financially.

Laurent was also working with several area construction companies to erect at Domain St-Buvard a series of tiny houses—made of stone and wood to blend in with the landscape of the *terroir*—for the families who worked the vineyard.

He was even talking about establishing scholarships for those young people interested in leaving the area to go on to university.

But as far as Maggie was concerned, the bottom line for all this titanic change in their lives was that Laurent was happier than Maggie had ever seen him. Busier too. From designing and building the single family dwellings on the property, to over-seeing his now much larger vineyard empire and teaching the families the skillsets needed to make a living, Laurent was always moving.

"I don't suppose it was a surprise that Laurent would want to enlarge his dominion," Grace said. "But he's really a mega landowner now, isn't he? That must please him."

Maggie smiled because she knew the truth was nowhere so simple. She knew what it had cost for Laurent to look at Domaine St-Buvard through a different prism, one that might not include a generation of grandsons running it or making enough profit for most people to consider worth doing. They'd had many long and intense conversations before he decided to buy up the surrounding vineyards.

And in the end, it had all come down to the realization that the value of the things that really mattered in life went beyond whether or not they made money. Laurent belonged to this land, this *terroir,* as much as if he'd been born here.

And Jemmy and Mila *had* been born here. To a Frenchman, there were few things as valuable.

A side bonus of Laurent's shifting his viewpoint on what he

wanted from the vineyard was the fact that now that he was no longer under the gun to be Laurent's heir apparent to Domaine St-Buvard, Jemmy had become fascinated with everything that happened in the vineyard. He had spent every waking hour of the spring and summer in the fields with Laurent and the people from the monastery, pruning, watering, and helping with all the chores leading up to the harvest.

Plus, there was now the new *boulangerie* in the village. In many ways Maggie thought that it was Laurent's wish to purchase and bring back the bakery that touched her more than anything else he'd done in the last six months.

Antoine Pelletier, a baker who had been living with his wife and two children at the monastery, now managed and ran the new village *boulangerie*. The apartment over the bakery had been renovated when the Americans owned the space two years earlier and now Antoine and his family lived there.

For Maggie, just walking through the village and seeing the *canelés* and the *éclairs* and *baguettes* in the display window once more was bittersweet. But in many ways it was her favorite part of Laurent's alchemy.

Laurent appeared at the door carrying a large basket of home-made garlic rounds and a bowl of *rouille*. Maggie's little terrier-poodle mix Petit Four ran out with him and jumped into Maggie's lap.

"Oh, just in time," Grace said. "It's been at least twenty minutes since we've eaten last. I was about to faint."

"You are ready for *l'apéro*?" Laurent asked, frowning at their watered-down coffees.

"Can we help?" Maggie said as she cuddled Petit-Four.

He leaned over and kissed her. "*Non*. Enjoy the afternoon."

Maggie noticed that he glanced out over the fields before he went back into the house. Regardless of how many workers he had who loved the vineyard almost as much as he did, he would always be drawn to it and its ever-changing landscape.

Maggie loved that about him.

Petit-Four jumped down and ran into the garden to chase voles. Maggie watched her go and realized she moved more stiffly than she used to. Like everyone else, she was getting old, Maggie thought sadly.

"Laurent worked a miracle with Zouzou," Grace said, glancing through the French doors at the two of them in the kitchen. "She's not only lost weight but she laughs now. I don't know how he did it."

The fact was, Laurent's magic touch had extended beyond whatever change he was able to bring about in Zouzou and his own worldview. After Grace and Zouzou returned to Atlanta last winter, he called Grace to tell her that he'd bought Eduard and Danielle's *mas* by the monastery and that if she were interested in living in St-Buvard again, he had an idea that might be profitable for her.

The Marceau *mas* was right off the main road that led to the village and the turn off that ran to the D9. The location was ideal if someone had the creative energy and desire to turn it into a bed and breakfast.

Grace jumped at the chance.

While Laurent owned the house, Grace ran the place in every aspect, from making the beds to designing each of the bedrooms and advertising for guests. Laurent worked with Zouzou whenever he had time to teach her to cook farmhouse meals. And Danielle worked at the *gîte* with Grace each morning to create true French breakfasts and to teach Zouzou what she knew about baking which was not Laurent's forte.

Danielle and Jean-Luc had decided to table their move to Nice, opting instead to sell Laurent the vineyard but stay in the house at least for now.

Maggie felt a warmth radiate throughout her as she thought of how things had worked out. It was a feeling that she could only describe as a deep, abiding contentment.

Everything was working out just as it was supposed to.

As for her parents, they had indeed moved to France and lived in an apartment in Aix just an hour away.

Maggie turned to Grace. "So how are things going back home?" she asked.

She knew that Taylor had opted to have her baby but refused to allow it to be put up for adoption. Within weeks of giving birth, she moved in with a friend but left the baby with her father and stepmother. Since Taylor hadn't dropped out of high school, Windsor was reluctant to push his luck. He and his wife Susie were in the process of adopting the infant. The last maternal thing Taylor did before leaving was name him Zircon.

"Windsor said Taylor wants to get her GED," Grace said with a sigh. "She wants to work in a tattoo parlor. But she didn't sound unhappy."

"It'll all get sorted out, Grace."

"Or it won't," Grace said with a wan smile. "Fix the things you can, right?" She nodded in the direction of Zouzou. "I'm not complaining. Things are good. How about you? Mom and Dad driving you crazy yet?"

Though in many ways the new situation was working out, Maggie's father continued to worsen with his moods vacillating between belligerent and euphoric to moments of extreme befuddlement. Her mother's French wasn't very good which served to add another level of stress to an already seriously stressful situation.

"I'm in Aix almost every day," Maggie admitted with a sigh. "Laurent and I think they'll need to move in here with us at Domaine St-Buvard before too long. It'll add a whole other level of chaos to our lives, what with the forty people working the fields pretty much twenty-four seven. Plus, Laurent is taking the kids out tomorrow to pick up a couple of puppies, if you can imagine. He says we need more dogs. And then there's my own work. I still have my newsletter to research, write and get out.

Which reminds me. I'm going into Arles this weekend to see if I can find any artists interested in advertising. Want to come? We could hit the flea markets early."

"Oh, yes! That would be perfect," Grace said, her eyes glowing with excitement. "I need to find an antique washstand."

When Maggie laughed, Grace joined in. "I know Laurent thinks all I have to do is throw cots in a room and provide clean towels and a basket of banana muffins but I want it to be pretty too."

"Of course you do. Don't listen to Laurent. As far as he's concerned, you could give your guests sleeping bags and it'd be fine as long as the food was good."

Laurent returned with two flutes of Prosecco and a small dish of olives.

"Don't listen to me about what?"

"Nothing, darling," Maggie said with a laugh as she took her glass. "God, you have hearing like a bat."

Humming, Laurent collected the coffee glasses and whistled for the little dog who came running and followed Laurent back inside the house. The sound of laughter from the vineyard added a patina of calm to the setting as Maggie turned to watch a small group of young people walking up and down the vineyard rows.

Laurent would announce the start of the harvest any day now. And then whatever relative calm they were experiencing would be gone in a whirlwind of action, excitement and hard work with everyone working to pick the grapes.

For the first time ever Maggie found herself actually looking forward to it.

"Oh!" she said, turning back to Grace. "What about Garner? Is he coming out to see you?"

"We've been talking about it," Grace said.

"He's retired so there would be no problem in him moving over here, right? If all the stars align?"

"In theory any way. I'm trying not to rush things."

Maggie wiped the condensation off her champagne glass. The sun was wavering in the sky as if undecided about whether or not to drop. She knew it wouldn't be long before she'd be glad of a sweater.

"It feels so weird seeing Madame Renoir's bakery open for business," Grace said. "If you remember, I nearly died in that bakery."

"I remember."

"Mind you, it doesn't stop me from going in there and loading up on their *chouquettes*."

Maggie laughed. "Of course not. Their *chouquettes* are the best."

"But still, it kind of feels like we've come full circle, you know?" Grace said. "Back to where we began?"

Maggie reached over and squeezed her best friend's hand.

"You took the words right out of my mouth," she said.

To follow more of Maggie's sleuthing and adventures in Provence, order **Murder in the Vineyard,** *Book 12 of the Maggie Newberry Mysteries!*

LAURENT'S RACLETTE

This is a perfect meal or snack for *après-ski* or even if you don't ski. Ideal for cold weather but I happen to know Laurent makes it in the fall and spring too.

You will need:
  2 pounds thin-skinned potatoes, scrubbed
  1 onion, peeled and thinly sliced
  1 TB lemon juice
  1 pound raclette cheese

Boil potatoes and simmer until they are tender when pierced, about 20 minutes.
  Mix onion slices with lemon juice.
  Drain cooked potatoes and put in a shallow 8x11-inch casserole pan.
  Slice raclette and arrange over top of potatoes. Broil until cheese melts.
  Eat with onion on the side and add pickles if desired. Salt and pepper to taste.

ABOUT THE AUTHOR

USA TODAY Bestselling Author Susan Kiernan-Lewis is the author of *The Maggie Newberry Mysteries,* the post-apocalyptic thriller series *The Irish End Games, The Mia Kazmaroff Mysteries,* and *The Stranded in Provence Mysteries,* and *An American in Paris Mysteries.* If you enjoyed *Murder in Grenoble,* please leave a review saying so on your purchase site.

Visit my website at www.susankiernanlewis.com or follow me at Author Susan Kiernan-Lewis on Facebook.

Made in the USA
Coppell, TX
04 October 2022